The Astonished Eye

To Pam —
with best wishes —

The Astonished Eye

TRACY KNIGHT

Five Star • Waterville, Maine

First Edition
First Printing: December 2003

Published in 2003 in conjunction with Tekno Books and
Ed Gorman.

Set in 11 pt. Plantin by Ramona Watson.

Printed in the United States on permanent paper.

Library of Congress Cataloging-in-Publication Data

Knight, Tracy.
    The astonished eye / by Tracy Knight.
      p. cm.
    "Five Star first edition titles"—T.p. verso.
    ISBN 1-59414-066-9 (hc : alk. paper)
    1. Unidentified flying objects—Fiction.   2. Human-alien
encounters—Fiction.   3. Journalists—Fiction.   4. Illinois—
Fiction.   I. Title.
PS3611.N57A87 2003
 813'.6—dc22   2003062360

Dedication

For Mom, Dad, and brother Bill, with whom I was
privileged to share the perfect nest, and who taught
me—through word and deed—about the magic

For Ed Gorman, Carol Gorman, and Peter Crowther,
who told me I had wings

And for Sharon Elizabeth, with whom I soar

Acknowledgements

Each of these amiable entities played a role in this novel's creation, though precious few are aware of it: Virginia Allison, Ray Bradbury, Gary Braunbeck, Mickey Carroll, Dr. James E. Coeur, Avery David, Peter Enfantino, Edith and Pat Ewing, Philip José Farmer, Susan Gleason, Martin Greenberg, Mae Jacobs, Dr. Susan Knight, Z. Knight, David Knowles, Randy Logan, Pat Metheny, Peggy Nadramia, Rob Nassif, Bill Nolden, Luanne Oleas, Karen Patterson, Rex Reu, Wayne Allen Sallee, Larry Segriff, Duane and Joyce Taylor, Susan Wilson, J. N. Williamson, Jeanne E. Westby, Dr. William Yabroff, and the City of Carthage, Illinois.

Introduction

By Philip José Farmer

I have read many hundreds of mystery and adventure, fantasy and science-fiction novels during my 85 years of life as a carbon-based form. (Never mind the silicon decades.) That I can still be intrigued by Tracy Knight's *The Astonished Eye* shows that he has something to say that's new and surprising and—sometimes—scary and mysterious.

The Astonished Eye is Knight's first novel, though not by any means his first published fiction. His short stories have been printed in books specializing in the mystery, science-fiction, suspense, and horror genres. These include anthologies such as *Werewolves*, *Whitley Strieber's Aliens*, *The UFO Files*, three books in the *Cat Crimes* series, and a chapter in the Writer's Digest book *Writing Horror*. His name and work also may be familiar from his column on Psychology and Crime Fiction for the *Mystery Scene* periodical.

I saw first-hand his knack for storytelling when this young man wrote an excellent next-to-last chapter for a limited-edition "round-robin rural romance and murder mystery" in which I took part: *Naked Came The Farmer*. This was not an easy feat since some of the writers had gone somewhat astray and their various sidetrack Odysseys and cowpath wanderings had to be assembled and set on the right path—channeled, if you will. Knight achieved this quite cleverly and logically. Cleverness and logic are often not the same thing, in romance or in mysteries.

In *The Astonished Eye*, Knight does not depend upon

free-flowing gore or gross-out mayhem to intrigue or shock readers. His voice is, usually, rather quiet or understated. Yet, it's effective.

Nor is the Kenneth Patchen quotation which is the sigil of this novel inappropriate.

The novel before you is not only about mysteries, it is about The Mystery. Mystery with the capital M is the essence of this work. The cosmos and the why and how and omega of the all are—even when not openly stated—the invisible threads of the weaving of this story. They deal with the sacred.

But the story and the characters come first in Tracy's book. And though some of these characters and story elements seem at first sight to be staples of the science-fiction/fantasy field, they are shown at a different angle or with an intriguing interpretation.

The twists and turns and perspectives Knight uses may stem from professional or geographical background. He practices clinical psychology in the small west-central Illinois town of Carthage and teaches at Western Illinois University. Despite his Ph.D. in psychology, he is very knowledgeable about people and has a deep sympathy and empathy for his patients—evident in his treatment of the characters in the book at hand.

Now, I hope I may be permitted a deviation or what may momentarily seem to be an irrelevant digression.

Part of this story deals with an Unidentified Flying Object, though it is different from other UFOs I've read about or seen in movies. I, however, know that such things as UFOs exist.

I don't necessarily mean by UFOs such things as spaceships operated by extraterrestrials or submerged Atlanteans. I mean that UFOs could be and most probably are quite natural terrestrial phenomena. But they likely are phenomena the origin and nature of which are as yet unknown to science. Perhaps electromagnetic in form. Perhaps hallucination-producing. Whatever their origin, some do exist. At least five percent of them remain stubbornly unexplained, and it seems possible that many of the so-called logical explanations of UFOs are illogical and don't really explain whatever it is that many human beings have seen.

Anyway, I—along with several hundreds of other people—saw a UFO one summer night over the skies of Peoria, Illinois, in the early 1950s. The U.S. Air Force claimed that it was a weather balloon. But weather balloons—or any kind of balloons—don't glow a bright blue, or stop suddenly and reverse their path, or dart off quickly at right angles, or circle or dive swiftly down and then ascend even more swiftly and then just disappear. So, I know that I—and many hundreds, and perhaps many more—observed the UFO and the observations were reported in the local newspaper. What I don't know is what caused this object to form or what force—electromagnetic or astronomical or meteorological—made it behave as it did.

It's one of those many mysteries that make up The Mystery.

I have made this slight digression or minor irrelevancy because I point out that what you may regard as fantasy in this work (many wonderful, awful things besides the UFO) may be true. It's just that we can't, as yet, explain them.

And maybe these unexplainable things or beings can't explain *us*.

Philip José Farmer
Peoria, IL

"Suddenly, one ordinary autumn day, an ordinary aspen leaf burnished with breathtaking luminescence falls within my ken. My stomach unknots, and something within me knows that death does not have final dominion."
—Sam Keen

"Life must go on;
I forget just why."
—Edna St. Vincent Millay

"Everything is full of gods."
—Thales of Miletus

"And I think there is nothing in the world but the Mystery."
—Kenneth Patchen

Prologue:

Infinity's Waifs

I.

The craft drifted lazily through the starry expanse, a glistening teardrop in the endless night. Inside, the entity pressed one hand against its face, attempting to recall what it looked like. It had been such a long time.

How long? How long since it had seen itself, or been seen?

No answer.

Its face felt smooth and symmetrical but as much as the entity tried, it could not conjure an image to accompany the shape traced by its touch.

Faceless.

It peered through the portal of the small craft. A planet came into view. How many did that make now? How many sojourns?

Just as no image had come to define its physical appearance, these questions went unanswered, left dangling in space like the milky smear of stars.

There was a purpose—that was certain—but if the entity had ever fathomed it, that knowledge had been forfeited, gone the way of its identity, its appearance, its life.

It understood only that as its ship streaked through the boundary of another world, something of consequence would happen: some balance would be struck, or wisdom gained.

And that's all that mattered, that *something* mattered.

Penetrating the atmosphere of the blue world, the craft shuddered.

The being lay back and closed its eyes.

Although there was no way to be certain, it thought it was smiling.

II.

The most hopeless case I've ever seen.

For the thousandth time since he'd run away from the foster home two days earlier, the caseworker's words erupted through Jeffrey Sprague's mind like a Roman candle.

The shadowed tree limbs wavered and danced as angry, fearful tears blurred his vision. He pulled his jacket more tightly around him, zipped it up to his neck. It was only early September, but the temperature was clearly testifying to autumn's imminent arrival. Jeffrey's breath came out as silver plumes, luminous in the dying moonlight.

It was after midnight. He wished morning would come.

Feeling a nuzzling on the back of his leg, he turned around, crouched and petted the friendly mutt who'd found him in the forest a few hours earlier. The dog was beige-colored, with long, matted fur that stuck out around the colorful knitted sweater it wore. Its tongue dangled from the side of his mouth when it panted. Moist brown eyes wide with pure anticipation, it wagged its tail and tipped its head to one side.

"That's a good boy," Jeffrey said, rubbing his hand back and forth across the dog's fur, which seemed to have captured and held any last traces of warmth in the world that night. "I'm so happy you found me. Been by myself so long. I was getting lonely."

Jeffrey stood up and peered through the dense, gloomy woods. It seemed like days since he'd realized he was lost. But now, ahead in the distance, dim light smudged the sky.

Perhaps there was a town just ahead.

That's where he'd go. Toward the light.

He took three steps and promptly tripped over a dead tree limb. His left knee hit the ground hard; flames of pain leapt up his leg. He cried out.

The mutt yelped softly—concerned—ran to Jeffrey and vigorously licked his face.

"Thanks," Jeffrey said, feeling stupid for falling down. He was twelve years old and throughout those years, he'd been called "misfit" and "loser" uncountable times. Whether it was due to the fact that he was a little slower than the other kids, or that his clothes weren't as new and tidy, or that he moved with the clumsiness that just now had made him fall, he'd been branded—especially since he'd been flung into the confusing world of foster care—as someone who wasn't part of the herd.

Alone.

But that wasn't the worst. *The most hopeless case I've ever seen.* That was the worst.

When he'd run away from the foster home in Keokuk two days earlier, a part of him knew that he was running away from the caseworker's words. Sure, there was the fact that he'd been in eleven foster homes in two years, each one contributing another little scar to his character, each one reminding him that he didn't quite fit, didn't quite belong, that there wasn't a place for him in this world.

But still. Those words.

The most hopeless case I've ever seen.

When Jeffrey was nine years old, his father died in a car accident during an ice storm, his car careening off Iowa Highway 218, crashing through a bridge railing and plummeting into the Mississippi River. Three agonizing days had passed before his body was found.

His mom had tried to carry on, tried her best to raise her only child, but soon Jeffrey was watching with horror as she spiraled downward, her sad descent fueled by the cancerous grief and the whiskey she drank every day to dull her torment.

One sunny May afternoon he'd burst into the house, skipping and shouting with joy, clutching a spelling paper on which he'd earned an A, confident that his little victory would bring a smile to his mother's wan lips.

He'd found her sitting in her recliner, dead, a long-ashed cigarette still smoldering between her fingers.

No smile would ever again cross Mom's lips. She wouldn't pat his head anymore and tell him what a good boy he was, or give him scraps of wisdom he could carry with him forever.

Within minutes, he had dashed to the garage—body ignited with shock and pain—grabbed a shovel and stumbled to the plush field out back where Dad and he had played catch so many times.

Determined to be the man of the house in the only way he could imagine, he convinced himself it was his duty to bury his mother. Once he began digging, though, a better idea came to him.

He dug a large hole, clambered into it, then began to bury *himself*. Sobbing and shouting, he scooped in enough warm black earth to cover himself up to the shoulders.

That was when he heard the plane flying overhead.

He had arched his neck to watch it sail across the sky. Bright sunlight reflected off its hull and smote his eyes, like a cosmic searchlight finding him there, noticing him. Somehow, that sight had splintered his trance. He went silent, letting the hot tears flow and the snot run. Resting his head upon the pile of earth that embraced him, he wept until his breath was almost gone. Then, exhaustion having cleansed him, Jeffrey wriggled out of his makeshift grave, returned to the house and called the ambulance.

The day of Mom's funeral, the State took guardianship, deciding they would become his parent. Soon it had become obvious they weren't up to the job. They placed him in foster homes where the parents simply didn't like him, sent him to schools where the kids taunted and tortured him, and transferred him whenever the least bit of trouble emerged.

The pattern of his life had become, at its base, a dance: placement in a new home; getting into a few fist fights on the schoolyard when teased, or breaking a window at church when despairing; a harsh, eye-glazing lecture from the caseworker; another placement; and then the cycle would begin anew.

He knew the dance as well as he knew the Pledge of Allegiance and, although he didn't want to be a bad kid, he was compelled to act out his part. It seemed to be the only role available.

Thinking of what he had become gave him a sickened feeling in the pit of his stomach. Jeffrey *knew* there was more inside him: there was a boy who had wept after he accidentally shot a sparrow with a BB gun; a boy who had picked up a flattened squirrel from the road, brought it home and buried it; a boy who had secretly left hand-picked wildflowers on the doorstep of every girl in his first-grade class one May Day.

There was a boy inside with a heart that tried to embrace the world with the same force with which the world pushed him away.

And so finally, two days ago, carrying nothing more than the clothes on his back, Jeffrey had slipped out the bedroom window of the Keokuk foster home and run like he'd never run before. Running without a clear goal or a finish line, unless it was a home that he'd long ago learned to fear even dreaming about. Or perhaps it was a new role he was searching for, the role of a nice boy of whom any parent could be proud.

Possibilities. Choices. Hope.

He gazed into the night sky, counting his breaths as he counted the stars. Both, it seemed that moment, were infinite.

The painful throbbing of his leg extinguished. The dog nuzzled him again, encouraging him to move on. As he walked through the forest, more carefully now, the only sounds he heard were the polite, muffled crackling of the twigs beneath his feet, the breeze breathing through the trees.

Suddenly a violet streak of light, high in the sky, caught Jeffrey's eye. It looked like a meteor but it was too brilliant, and it moved with a grace and measured speed inconsistent with a plummeting rock.

It traced a wide, blazing arc across the night and disappeared in the distance.

Not that far away.

Jeffrey crouched and put his arms around the stray dog who'd adopted him. The dog licked him, its tongue tugging Jeffrey's face into a half-smile.

"That was a falling star, boy," Jeffrey said, pulling the dog closer and hugging it tightly, feeling its warm breath against his cheek. "That means we get a wish."

Part One
The Last Munchkin

Chapter One

Of fortune he had little; of luck, even less.

Ben Savitch knew he could have that precise sentence chiseled into a lustrous granite headstone tomorrow and it would still be pertinent when the time came for him to slumber forever in Cadaver City, the Carcass Center, the Corpse Chateau.

It wasn't that he was a pessimist. Not really. He'd just lived inside this particular sack of flesh long enough to hazard a few temperate predictions. So it didn't surprise Ben Savitch that, upon arriving at the small Midwestern town he hadn't seen in over thirty-five years, what happened happened.

This is what happened.

Approaching the city limits of Elderton, Illinois, he took a last sip of the Bud he'd kept clutched between his legs for the past fifteen miles, then pitched the can out the window. It clattered and danced and flipped across the fragmented, bumpy two-lane highway, nearly braining a roadside raccoon which was standing on its hind legs, bewitched by the passing metal beast.

Ben smiled as he crossed the boundary marked by the green city limits sign—ELDERTON POP. 1523—entirely expecting that long-sequestered childhood memories would blossom full-flowered into a bouquet of nostalgia.

Nothing.

He gazed upon the modest, clean streets lined with lordly oaks and elms and maples and pines, the unassuming yet tidy homes, each with its own porch swing drifting lazily in the breeze. Nothing came to mind.

Nothing.

He didn't recognize one thing. Not a corner or a building or a street sign or a storefront or a schoolhouse.

He frowned. Elderton looked like any other little Midwestern town, albeit less decayed than many he'd passed through. He felt no connection, no tether.

While formulating a proper series of curse words to reflect his surprise and disappointment, suddenly—out of the corner of his right eye—he glimpsed a light brown blur.

The car lurched as he desperately spun the steering wheel.

A sickening thump. A brief, strangled yelp.

Wincing, he glanced into his rearview mirror.

Shit. He'd run over a dog. It was lying on its right side, thrashing its legs like it thought it was still running.

He slowed his rust-red Honda Civic and, against every city-born instinct, pulled to the side of the road.

Great, Ben thought. *The very first thing I do upon returning to the town I haven't seen since I was six years old is hit a dog. That's just like me.*

It was true. It fit the plot line of Ben's existence with immaculate perfection. The only exciting things that ever happened to him typically involved a serious mishap—or, more often, a series of mishaps. Take his lackluster career as a journalist. Take his three failed marriages. *Please.*

On the highway of life, Ben was the man tooling down an eternal straightaway, left turn signal perpetually blinking. Always maintaining the appearance of going somewhere, of arriving at a meaningful destination, showing every outward intention of making the turns he needed to make. But never doing it, never even noticing the hopeful roads available to him. Never taking the turn.

Yes, the left-blinker driver. That was him.

With a resigned though impatient sigh, he opened the door and stepped out into the balmy autumn day. He took a deep breath of the crisp, invisible air and steadied himself. As he walked toward the dog, the first thing that grabbed Ben's attention was that although it was still early September, the beige-colored mutt was clad in a colorfully festive sweater, something a spoiled hound would wear, embarrassed, on Christmas Day. Knitted splashes of red, purple, yellow and green festooned the dog's body, in stark contrast to the dark blood now pooling around it.

Great, it couldn't have been a mangy, unwanted stray. Oh no. It had to be a winsome spinster's pampered little Boo-Boo.

As if appearing from nowhere, a crowd began to gather. At least seven or eight people shambled to the curb, their eyes uniformly darting back and forth between Ben and the dog, who let out a horrid, yielding, final moan, then joined the autumn silence.

That's what Ben noticed most of all during his first ghastly moments back in Elderton: the silence. In Chicago, everything was honking horns and swearing cabbies, grousing pedestrians and shrieking sirens. Not here. It was so quiet he heard the toe of an old lady's shoe scraping against the dying grass as she nervously watched the scene. He heard an old man's dry swallow, and a little boy's muffled sob.

He furtively hoped one of the faces in the crowd would be familiar, perhaps a teacher he'd had in school or a Little League coach or a kindly Cub Scout leader: someone who would step forward, introduce himself with a smile, and lend a gracious hand to the long-lost Ben Savitch.

Nothing.

The quietly sobbing boy, not much more than ten years

old, stepped to the front of the congregating crowd, then off the curb and into the street. He adjusted the Chicago Cubs cap that perched crookedly on his head, hiding most of his flame-red hair. He tugged at the waist of his dirty jeans and scuffed a shoe against the pavement. Tears shimmered in his Caribbean blue eyes. The boy seemed to want to say something, but his trembling lips prevented it.

A very short older man traipsed over and laid his hand on the boy's shoulder. The man couldn't have stood more than five feet tall. He rubbed one sausage-fingered hand over his bald head, squinted sympathetically at the boy, then raised his eyes to meet Ben's.

"You hit the dog," the little man said.

Having lived in Chicago for the past twenty years, Ben had to consciously prevent himself from flailing his arms like a Dexedrined traffic cop and yelling: *What do I look like? Some kind of retarded geek? I know I hit a dog, you putz!*

Instead he said, softly, "Yeah. I know."

"That was my dog," the boy managed, his voice a cracking squeak. "I only found him two days ago. He was my friend. He liked me."

Ben took a few steps toward the boy, spreading his hands before him. "I'm sorry, son. I really am." *Jesus Christ, let this nightmare be over.*

Shaking his head, the little bald man said, "That's the first animal I've seen killed like this . . . well, gee, *ever.*"

Ben opened his mouth, prepared to air his disbelief, but stopped himself. After all, he was here to investigate a story, a story that might catapult him into the loftiest tier of professional journalism. There would be no value in alienating potential sources.

What surprised him most was when the rest of the shuffling crowd, not to mention several more people only now arriving, nodded and muttered their assent.

"Yep, that's right, Almo. Never heard of no animal being run over, hit like that."

"Sure hasn't happened in *my* time."

"Nope. Not even a squirrel, nor a rabbit."

"I can't believe it. Just . . . can't . . . believe it."

"What do you suggest we do?" Ben asked, trying to sound as gentle and compassionate as possible, even though at that moment he wished he could channel Moe Howard and perform a proper crowd-smack, just one big long slap across the slack cheeks of the whole damned lot of them.

The little bald man cocked one straggly eyebrow, then put a hand to his hip. "You're on the deck of the Titanic," he said to Ben, eyes beseeching in their clarity. "What do you want to do now?"

"Huh?" Just what a guy needed when he was looking for a little support: a bald pygmy's psychotic philosophy. "What do you mean?" Ben added, positing that the implication of his *huh* hadn't fully registered with the diminutive humanoid.

The little man shrugged. "That's the question. That's *always* the question. You're on the deck of the Titanic. What do you want to do now?"

"Jump?" Ben said, shrugging too.

The little man shrugged again.

Jesus. I'm having a shrugging showdown with a deranged midget.

Silence swelled until it seemed ready to detonate.

Then the little man, perhaps taking pity on Ben, said, "Well . . . gosh, let's see." He scratched his shiny scalp as if he were computing a calculus problem. "I reckon it's the boy's dog, so he oughta be involved."

"Yeah, that's it," another man piped in, raising his hand

27

skyward like a schoolboy impatient to please. "This man here that hit the dog, he can bury it . . . *with* the boy."

Someone gasped and said, "You don't mean that he should bury the boy *with* the dog."

"Of course not, Milo. He and the boy can bury the poor dog . . . *together.*"

"Ahhhhh."

Again, everyone nodded and murmured agreeably.

Ben half-expected the crowd to erupt into applause, cheers, eardrum-piercing two-fingered whistles.

Before Ben had a chance to devise a clean, crisp, face-saving escape, the little man had waddled into a nearby house and returned, smiling and holding a nice clean shovel in his hand. He presented it to Ben proudly, as if he were bestowing an enchanted sword upon a wayward prince.

Ben grabbed it. He was speechless. Then he looked down at the boy. There weren't any options left. "Well, son, do you want to come with me?"

"To bury my dog?"

No, to give a lecture on cold fusion at MIT. To kick-dance with the Rockettes at Radio City Music Hall. To pick up a couple of girls and knock back highballs until we achieve incoherence.

"Yeah," Ben said. "To bury your dog."

The boy wiped his eyes free of tears and tried on a quivering smile. "Sure."

As Ben opened his trunk, the little man called, "Mister, you remember to bring me back my shovel. Okay? Please?"

Ben nodded, gritting his teeth in a smile so tense he thought he might grind an incisor to powder. With an exaggerated reverence intended as sarcasm, he shifted his overnight bag to one side and placed the shovel across the width of the car at the back of the trunk.

Then he turned and gathered up the dog's broken body. As he cradled the blood-soaked frame in his arms, Ben realized that he'd never before held a dead animal. The moment seized something inside him and twisted. Not good.

The dog's lusterless, drying eyes looked into and out at nothingness. Its tongue lolled between bared teeth as if, in the moment before it died, it had owned an ephemeral notion to bite Death in the bony ass. Ben felt fleeting admiration for such an attitude.

Carefully he laid the dog's body right next to the nice clean shovel and slammed the trunk lid.

Apparently satisfied by Ben's gesture of responsibility, the crowd began to disperse.

Ben and the boy got into the car. As he started the engine, Ben glanced through the windshield, up into the cloudless blue sky.

God, why don't you just hurtle a big God-sized piano down this way and smash me into a hairy flapjack, okay? Just get it over with.

Nothing.

It figured. God always avoided the easy way out. If Ben's life proved anything, it was that God opted for leisurely torture.

If there were an afterlife, the first thing Ben planned to do when he arrived was to grab God by his Godly lapels, yank Him so close he could smell God-breath, and demand some answers.

He shoved the gearshift into Drive and off they went to bury the dead dog, sweater and all.

Ben had come to Elderton—to the town he had known as home from birth to age six—because of the anonymous tip he'd received that a UFO had crashed nearby. What a coup! Who better than a hometown boy to infiltrate a godforsaken rural hamlet and coerce it into disgorging its secrets?

But instead of interviewing townspeople or scouring the countryside in search of an extraterrestrial spacecraft, he had a crying little boy in his car, and they were going to bury a dead dog.

A damned dead dog.

In a damned sweater.

Chapter Two

"My name's Ben Savitch," the man said, his attention riveted to the road. He hadn't so much as flicked his eyes in Jeffrey's direction since they'd driven away from the crowd, almost like he was mad or something. Jeffrey had been ignored by masters in the art and so recognized an uninterested opening conversational gambit.

He paused for a moment. This, he realized, would set the tone for their relationship—to offer the chance for what passed for friendship between young and older people or to leave Ben as no better than a social worker.

Jeffrey's life had been short, but full of opportunities to learn about human nature. To his surprise, Elderton was accepting him uncritically. A blind eye had been turned to him sleeping in a barn on the outskirts of town, or on the pews of local churches. Plates of food had been left in oddly conspicuous places where he could take them, knowing he should not feel guilty. Folk on the streets courteously ignored him as though they were waiting for him to make the first move. He had felt weird but increasingly happy—particularly after talking with Almo.

But now, this new pain of loss . . . forcing him to make choices. Jeffrey appraised the man, who looked oddly worn even though he was only middle-aged, probably the same age as his Dad had been when he died. His chestnut hair was paling into dull gray—and more of the whiskers on his unshaven chin were white than brown. The lattice of wrinkles sketched on his face hinted he did more frowning than smiling.

Nonetheless, he was fit-looking, trim and somewhat muscular. A strong, unhappy man by the looks of him.

Jeffrey then figured out that he should probably tell the man his name, too. "I'm Jeffrey Sprague." The words, "Nice to meet you" cautiously left the gate open.

"Sooooo," Ben said, stretching out the word. "Where do you think we should bury your dog?"

Having only arrived in town two days before, Jeffrey wasn't really familiar with the area. He looked through the windshield at the passing fields of dying corn, and gestured toward the first corner he saw.

"There," he said, pointing to a gravel road that ran alongside a decrepit roller skating rink. "Turn there."

Ben sighed, flicked on his left turn signal, and took the turn. "Okay, that's fine," he said, "just point out where you want to do this. We can get it over with and I can take you home."

Jeffrey fell silent.

"You *do* live here in town, don't you?"

"Well . . ."

"It doesn't matter," Ben said. "Tell you what: wherever you live, I'll drive you home. Even if it's Havana. Havana, *Illinois,* that is." Ben laughed but it was a weak one.

"To be honest," Jeffrey said, "I don't really live around here. Don't live anywhere at all."

"What?"

"Well, see . . ." He hesitated. "Promise you won't tell nobody?"

Ben's forehead furrowed. A few long, stray eyebrow hairs protruded at attention. "Sure. I promise."

"I'm a foster kid. Both my parents are dead. Been in a whole bunch of foster homes and . . . well, I just couldn't take it anymore. I was sad all the time. Ran away."

"Sorry to hear that," Ben said.

Jeffrey didn't detect any concern in Ben's voice.

"There!" Jeffrey shouted suddenly, pointing.

Ben jammed on the brakes. The Civic skidded in the gravel, its rear end fishtailing.

"What?" Ben asked. For the first time since they'd gotten into the car, he made eye contact with Jeffrey. Jeffrey had looked into lots of eyes, searching for someone who would care. This man's eyes were blanker, flatter, than Jeffrey expected a grown-up's to be. He'd always hoped that, when he grew up, life would grow stronger, so strong it would shine from his eyes.

He continued pointing toward the corner of a cornfield at the intersection of two gravel roads. "There," he said, "there's where we can bury my dog."

"Oh. Yeah." Ben nodded, popped the latch to release the trunk lid, and got out of the car.

Jeffrey followed him.

The fishtailing had slapped the corpse around, splattering the overnight bag with blood and other less identifiable fluids.

Ben hesitated before carefully slipping his hands under the dead dog.

"Mister . . . Ben . . . you aren't going to tell nobody that I ran away, are you?" Jeffrey asked. "I mean, if you do they'll put me in another foster home. I won't be happy ever again."

Looking like he might throw up as he lifted the dog's corpse, Ben shook his head. "No, I won't tell anybody. But you have to figure out what you want to do. You can't just live in the streets, even in a little town like Elderton. I wish I could help you, but . . ."

Head turned slightly to one side to avoid either the smell

or the sight, Ben carried the dog's body to the corner and laid it down in the grass. Then he walked slowly back to the trunk and grabbed the shovel.

"Do you live in Elderton?" Jeffrey asked. He would have guessed not. Ben Savitch seemed different from anyone Jeffrey had encountered since arriving. Everyone here was calm and kind. Ben seemed rough around the edges, even surly.

"Used to," Ben said, kicking the shovel's blade into the ground and overturning patches of rich black earth, one by one. "My family lived here when I was little."

Jeffrey let moments pass, watching the man digging. The look on Ben's face told Jeffrey that the man was wishing he was anywhere else in the universe but there, doing anything else in the universe other than what he was doing.

"Is it a nice town?"

Having cleaved a small, grave-shaped rectangle from the top layer of soil, Ben began putting his back into it, excavating shovelfuls of crumbly loam, some of which held writhing earthworms, agitated to find their cozy home invaded.

"Is it a nice town?" Ben echoed. "I can't really tell you. Even though I lived here for six years, I can't say I remember a lot about the town, except that it was quiet."

"Yeah. Quiet." Jeffrey smiled.

"Have you made any friends yet?"

Was the man really interested or just making small talk? Jeffrey couldn't tell.

"One," Jeffrey said proudly. "That man who was with me back there when you hit . . . when the accident happened."

"Oh, yes. The short guy?"

"Yeah. That's Almo Parrish. And you know something?"

Ben was beginning to pant now, having shoveled at least two feet into the ground. "What?" he managed between ragged breaths.

"He's the last Munchkin."

"The what?"

"The last Munchkin. You know that movie, *The Wizard of Oz*?"

"Sure."

"He's the last Munchkin from that movie who's still alive. He's almost a movie star. Well, I guess he *is* a movie star. And he told me I'd be safe here. He said Elderton is soft and magical."

"A nice person to have made friends with," Ben said, not a lick of interest or curiosity in his tone. Maybe all the work had stolen his energy.

A moment later, Ben pulled the shovel from the ground, thrust it blade-first into the earth and wiped his brow, a small smile of satisfaction on his face. "There," he said. "All done. Now to get your pooch in there."

"I'll help you," Jeffrey said, kneeling next to the dog's body and gently stroking its face. In recent months, this empathic mutt had been the only creature to show un-questioning love to Jeffrey. He wouldn't soon forget it.

"He was a good boy," Jeffrey whispered, and let it go at that.

Ben picked up the head end of the dog, Jeffrey its back end, and the two slowly lowered it into the shallow grave.

It fit perfectly.

"I'd like to say a few words," Jeffrey said, "if that's okay."

An expression of impatience flitted across Ben's face, then vanished just as quickly. "Sure," he said.

Jeffrey clasped his hands in front of him, bowed his

head, and said, "I just want to thank you for finding me. I was lost, but somehow when you joined up with me, I didn't feel that way no more. Felt like I belonged. And even though we didn't get to spend much time together as it turned out, I'll still remember you as long as I live, even when I get real old. Promise. I hope I see you in heaven someday. I hope you'll save a place for me." He paused, then: "Amen."

"Amen," Ben said, wiping one palm against the other. "Good job. Now just let me finish this up and we'll be on our way."

Moving quickly, Ben Savitch filled in the grave of the nameless dog who wore the colorful sweater. Within thirty seconds, he was patting down the mound of soil.

It looked good to Jeffrey. Peaceful.

"Shall we go?" Ben said, turning toward the car and walking away.

"Sure," Jeffrey said. "Thanks."

After the shovel had been returned to the trunk, Ben and Jeffrey got into the Civic. Just as Ben turned the key and the engine cranked to life, Jeffrey asked, "Where you taking me now?"

"Wherever you want to go," Ben answered, making a U-turn at the intersection.

"Don't know where I want to go."

"Well, you have a few minutes to think about it."

Jeffrey decided to delay by making more conversation. "Say, Ben, why did you come back? Just to visit?"

"Kind of. Actually, I'm in Elderton to work on a story. I'm a journalist, a reporter."

"Like one of those guys on TV, or like you write for the *Weekly Reader* or something?"

"Not exactly. I *am* a writer, but not for a big newspaper. I mean, it's big, but—"

"But what? You mean like that *New York Times* or something?"

"No. I write for *The Astonished Eye*."

"Hmmm." Jeffrey tried his best to sound like he knew what the man was talking about.

Ben shifted uncomfortably in his seat. "It's . . . well, it's what they call a tabloid newspaper. We sell millions through subscriptions, grocery stores, newsstands, that sort of thing. We cover . . . real interesting stories."

Why was the man blushing?

"I see. So why are you in Elderton?"

Ben laughed nervously. "Because I got a tip that a UFO had crashed near here."

"Really? A UFO?"

"Really. But who knows whether the tip was true or not."

"It *was* true. It *is* true. At least I think it is."

For the second time since they'd met, Ben looked over at Jeffrey and this time really seemed to see him.

"It was?" Ben said. "How do you know?"

" 'Cause I saw it come down. Me and the dog. When we were in the forest."

They were nearing Elderton's courthouse square. Ben's eyes darted back and forth. He pressed an index finger to his lips.

"Did you see where it went down?"

"Kinda."

"You know something, Jimmy—"

"Jeffrey."

"Jeffrey. I think I'd like to talk to you a lot more about this. Maybe we can look for the UFO together. How does that sound to you? You think you could show me where it landed?"

Noticing the car slowing, Jeffrey had more immediate concerns. "Where you taking me?"

"I was thinking. I can pick you up in the morning, maybe take you to breakfast and we can talk about this—"

"Where you taking me?"

Ben cleared his throat. "I thought I'd see if there's a State office in town. See if I can find—I don't know—a social worker or something. They'll know what to do."

It was sheer instinct upon hearing the words "social worker."

Luckily the Civic had almost come to a full stop, so when Jeffrey threw open the car door and leapt out, it was easy to get his footing.

"Hey!" Ben Savitch shouted. "Kid! Come back here!"

By then, Jeffrey was half a block away.

He felt the same way he felt when he had run away from threatening bullies, or run away from his dead mother, or run away from loveless foster homes. It was as if his body had suddenly filled up with rocket fuel. As he ran, he felt like a superhero whom no one could ever capture.

It felt like his life depended on it.

It felt like he was flying.

Chapter Three

"You should have stayed put at the *Peoria Journal-Star*, Ben. I can't believe you're in—where?—Evanston, Illinois, chasing down little gray bulb-heads piloting flying cowflops."

Ben glowered, then held the telephone's handset at arm's length and gave it the finger.

"Not Evanston, Illinois," Ben said. "*Elderton*, Illinois. Why are you laughing? You sound like a braying ass, Max, just so you know."

He was sitting on the hard bed in the cinder-block room he'd checked into at the PrairieView Motel ("fifteen dollars a night; twelve-fifty if you make your own bed"), a one-story brick building containing fifty less-than-basic rooms situated on the west edge of town.

Spread across the bed were his laptop computer, a tangle of legal pads, pens (half of them dry), mounds of blue jeans and casual shirts and underwear, and several dog-eared books. In one corner, his newly washed overnight bag was drying next to the air conditioner. Long ago he'd christened his decorating style Rhodes Squalor: the unmistakable mark of the educated slob. He had coined that term to defend himself against the judgment of his second ex-wife, Darla. She hadn't bought it.

"El . . . der . . . ton," he repeated into the phone, drawing out each syllable as if Max were the village idiot. "It's a little town, downstate, west-central Illinois, a few miles east of the Mississippi River. And I can't believe you think I'd be better off at the *Journal-Star*. Hell, besides mastering the ancient art of writing obits, I was going nowhere fast."

Right after checking in, he'd called his friend Max Thomason for a couple of reasons: because he and Max had attended Columbia together and he liked to stay in touch with his former classmate, and because whenever he spoke to his friend who had become the most prosperous television journalist in Chicago, it accorded Ben a little shot glass of confidence that he too might someday make it big. Or, at least, make it. Today, his strategy was proving awkwardly ineffective.

Max remained silent for a moment, then said, "Ben, you've got so much potential—"

"Jesus Christ, Maxipad! You're talking to me like you're my mother or an alcoholic guidance counselor."

"Sorry, buddy. But I know how well you can write, what you can do when you're inspired. How long have you been with the *Eye*?"

"Six months."

"Given your work history, doesn't that mean you're about ready to insult the entire editorial staff and take a hike, move on to greener—yet equally turd-filled—pastures?"

Ben felt his nostrils flare to approximately the diameter of dinner plates. He wished that instead of calling Max, he'd called one of his ex-wives. At least their contempt was pure, unsullied by the etiquette of friendship.

Struggling to maintain his calm, Ben took a deep, slow breath before saying, "Not this time. I'm staying put for a while. Besides paying me obscenely well, I get to call my shots more often than I've ever been able to before, to follow the leads I consider promising. That means something to me, Max. I thought you'd understand."

"Sure I do, buddy. Sure I do."

With every syllable Max uttered, his voice sounded more condescending, disgustingly parental. Ben tasted acid creeping up from his stomach, a reverse lava flow.

Gulping down the liquid heat, Ben said, "Maybe this story will be the one, Max. You know me: ever hopeful." He chuckled, but it died a quick death.

Max began laughing so loudly that Ben had to hold the phone away from his ear. While holding it there, he shot it another bird.

"Hopeful?" Max said. "You? Hopeful? Good God, Ben, if you were any more hope*less,* you'd have a coffin laid out in a pre-dug grave, a priest on retainer, a shovel in hand, set to bury yourself, just to be prepared for your imminent demise."

Ben couldn't conceive an immediate rejoinder to that. Instead he said, "You laugh now, Maxipad, but think about it. If this is a bona fide crash of an extraterrestrial spacecraft and I cover it—turn up irrefutable physical evidence—it's my one-way ticket to the big leagues."

This wasn't going like Ben had thought it would, not at all. He had imagined that Max would give him a verbal pat on the shoulder, some hearty encouragement, all of the things one had a right to expect from an old and trusted friend. Instead, all Ben could hear was the sneer in Max's voice as he snickered at Ben's newest tabloid adventure.

"Yeah, well, you just wait, buddy boy!" Ben shouted into the phone. "I'll be picking up a bushel basket full of UFO fragments, maybe even interviewing its pilot, while you're up there in Chicago, covering . . . I don't know . . . whatever it is you cover up there. Murder. Political corruption. Gang warfare. Your work will pale, Maxipad, compared to a story of a recovered UFO."

He slammed down the phone, hoping that Max would forget the exchange by the next time Ben needed him.

The funny thing was that Ben didn't even believe what he'd told his college pal. He knew the chances of this UFO crash being anything more than the pot-driven phantasm of a flying saucer fanatic were teensy. Just like the story of the Bigfoot who had been photographed watching television in a Missouri trailer home. Or the image of the Virgin Mary appearing in a taco salad at a pub in Indianapolis. Or the boy in Cedar Rapids whose family claimed that he bled supernaturally, exhibiting stigmata mirroring the wounds Gary Gilmore sustained when he was executed by a Utah firing squad. Or the channeler who claimed to be in direct contact with the unquiet spirit of Fats Waller, offering as proof the fact that he could sing "Your Feet's Too Big" with reasonable acumen. Or the man who lost over three hundred pounds within thirteen days by eating only black beans and Rice Krispies and drinking his own urine.

Of course, there was that boy, Johnny. Or was it Jimmy? Jerome? *He'd* said the UFO crash was real.

Naaaaaa.

"Oh, well," Ben said, getting up and walking to the large picture window. "Night has fallen in beautiful Elderton, Illinois. I wonder what kind of wildly stimulating things are happening here tonight."

He grabbed the metal pole hanging from the curtain rod and yanked it to one side.

He had never come as close to fainting as he did that moment.

Inches outside the window, eerily illuminated by the bruise-colored parking lot lights encircling the motel, was a man.

Standing at least six-feet-five, the man wore overalls that

42

hung from only one strap, no shirt beneath them. "Unkempt" would have been a polite assessment of the man's appearance, "filthy" more accurate. His greasy black hair vibrated stiffly in the breeze. Even in the faint glow of the mercury vapor lights, the man's face, his hollowed-out cheekbones, were obviously as pale as milk.

That wasn't the worst of it. Bad enough that Ben's first hours in a run-down Mom-and-Pop motel would be interrupted by a window-peeker who looked like a refugee from *Deliverance.*

But besides being obviously pale and filthy, the man was also obviously blind. Obscured and encrusted as though a film of frost covered them, his milky eyes wandered independently in their sockets, bobbing up, down, left, right at random.

Ben couldn't move. He wasn't scared in the sense of feeling threatened, but the sight was so damned weird. Unsettling. Feathers of unease grazed the back of his neck.

The tall blind man reached out and extended his index finger. Then, with exquisite daintiness, he tapped a dirty fingernail against the picture window . . .

tap

tap

tap

. . . and smiled, disclosing poorly spaced, rotten teeth.

"What do you want?" Ben said, so softly he knew the man couldn't hear him.

The blind man curled his right hand nearly into a fist, then wiggled his wrist up and down. A tiny, chilling wave. He mouthed some words, but Ben couldn't make them out.

"That's it!" Ben shouted, having recovered whatever stability he usually owned. He swept the curtain closed, marched to the door, and opened it.

"Listen, mister!" he began, pointing an accusing finger, then stopped.

No one stood there. The autumn breeze whistled through nearby trees, singing to the harvest moon that hovered in the sky, illuminating wispy clouds as they skittered past its face. The parking lot was barren save for Ben's Civic.

Beyond that, Ben saw nothing.

Nothing.

"Just as I thought," Ben said, hearing rare weakness and insecurity in his voice, "there's no excitement in Elderton tonight."

He closed the door and tried to laugh it off.

But he knew he would have trouble sleeping that night.

Chapter Four

"It's almost midnight. Which leaf do you think will be the first to fall?" The bright-eyed second-grader tugged at the sleeve of the eight-year-old girl standing next to him. "Which one?"

The little girl, blonde, face glowing with anticipation, whispered, "Shush. There's millions of leaves. You know that. There's only one person who knows which leaf will be the first to fall." She crossed her arms and tapped her foot, expressing impatience at the boy's silly question.

The citizens of Elderton filled the enormous yard surrounding the courthouse, awaiting the descent of the first autumn leaf. Older people tended to relax on the green wrought-iron benches generously placed along the sidewalks encircling the courthouse square. Children climbed on the large boulder sitting near the courthouse's south entrance, upon which a plaque stated that Abraham Lincoln had spoken there more than a century before. Most Eldertonians, however, stood shoulder to shoulder, talking quietly among themselves as they waited.

The courthouse was an imposing structure, by far the most impressive building in town. Fashioned of white Bedford stone, the three-story construction featured small red domes at each corner of its roof of Spanish tiles, then a gigantic red dome extending from its center, reaching for the sky. Atop the uppermost dome was a statue of white marble, a blindfolded woman holding a scale in one hand, a book in the other. She faced southward, eternally promising justice to the Confederacy following the Civil War. The courthouse looked as majestic and pristine as any castle, serving as a noble centerpiece to the little kingdom of Elderton.

The night sky was a palette of muddy cotton balls backlit by the lemon moon. The leaves had begun turning earlier in the week, winking with sleepy eyes of gold and orange that were visible even with only the street lights and stray flashlight beams to illuminate them. The cool breeze gently breathed away memories of summer.

The entire town had been loitering in the courtyard since a little before midnight, as they did every year upon receiving the call.

The bells in the courthouse tower tolled twelve times.

An excited child's voice: "There he is!"

The fifteen hundred twenty-three residents of Elderton turned their heads in unison.

Stepping around the corner of Main and Wabash was Almo Parrish, the last Munchkin. In the past, everyone knew he was near because he would arrive singing "We're Off to See the Wizard," skipping along at a sprightly pace belying his years.

Not tonight.

Tonight he walked with his head bowed, outwardly lost in a fog of worry.

Almo Parrish was a few whispers under five feet tall. His bald head was ringed with neatly clipped chestnut hair. His largish nose sat in the middle of a pixie face. Tonight that face was wrenched into a mask of concern.

"What's the matter?" someone asked.

No one answered. The crowd remained silent, focused upon Almo as he scuffled toward the makeshift stage set up near the north steps of the grand old courthouse.

Mayor Lewis Huston, clad in a shiny tuxedo and top hat, picked up the microphone and tapped it three times, then blew air into it. "Can you hear me? Good. Ladies and

Gentlemen, as always you didn't have much advance notice that this annual gathering was occurring tonight and, as has been the case the past fifteen years we've held this celebration, everyone came. I think we can consider the phone tree we set up last year a resounding success. As Mayor, that makes me proud. This is one of those special moments we have every year during which we remind ourselves what a true community is, when we share and commemorate the magic only we know."

Polite applause. Everyone's attention remained riveted upon the last Munchkin, shadows of disquiet now darkening their faces, too.

"And now, as you can all well see, our Master of Ceremonies has arrived. He's one of Elderton's most illustrious citizens. The last surviving member of the cast of little people in *The Wizard of Oz*, the man who embodies all the magic and hope that only a Munchkin can. Ladies and Gentlemen, I give you the last Munchkin . . . Almo Parrish!"

Mayor Huston adjusted his top hat as he stepped back from the microphone.

Amidst a rising wave of applause, Almo slowly ascended the steps of the makeshift stage, then finally looked up to take in the faces of the assembled citizens. His eyes brightened a bit, almost as though, until that moment, he hadn't noticed the people were there. He slid a footstool behind the lectern, then stepped up behind the microphone.

"Good evening," he said. There was a small echoing squeak, feedback from the speakers on the stage. Mayor Huston busily adjusted the volume knob.

"It's a blessing to see all of you tonight," Almo said. "We were all together for this celebration about a year ago, the last time we awaited the fall of the first autumn leaf. This last year has been a long one, and yet so woefully short. Aren't they all?"

The crowd fell into a cozy silence, now regarding Almo with a mixture of awe and respect.

Almo reached up with one hand and rubbed his eyes. "My friends, you know me. You know that whatever little magic I possess—*we* possess—has brought us nothing but smiles and laughter, the way all good magic does, the way Elderton's magic does. However, I come to you tonight telling you that I see distressing clouds on our horizon. For so many years we have reveled in the simple poetry of our quiet lives, the peace so many pursue and so few truly find. For that we should be grateful. But today . . . today there is something slouching toward our gentle town, toward all of us. Fellow citizens of Elderton, we are going to be invaded."

As if on cue, a few people in the audience gasped. But only a few. The rest seemed merely fascinated and not the least bit worried.

"Our town will be invaded by something unlike anything we have seen before. And we must band together, to recognize and celebrate our bonds as we never have before. Or our subtle magic shall perish. And with it . . . us."

A lone voice from the crowd: "Does this have somethin' to do with that ship that crashed out near Lou Bentley's farm?"

"I think so," said the last Munchkin, nodding. "I think it does. Soon I'll go have a look-see. But for now, this moment . . . this very moment is *our* time, my friends!"

All was silent for another few seconds. Then Almo Parrish, the last Munchkin, raised his head and narrowed his eyes as if he were hearing a distant song or divining the fingers of a far-off god going about its work.

He hopped off the stage and marched through the crowd, which then turned and followed him, a stream of humanity trailing him off the courthouse square and down Main Street. As one, they marched behind the last Munchkin—one block, two—until he reached the base of an ancient maple tree that stood majestically at the corner of Main and Fayette as it had for countless decades.

Clasping his hands in front of him, bowing his head, Almo waited for the crowd to arrive, to quiet themselves, to find their places in a grand circle around the tree.

They did. Again, absolute silence.

Then in one confident, dramatic sweep of his arm, he pointed upward, toward the top of the tree.

Everyone's head lifted, following the trail of his stubby finger. Several people trained their flashlight beams on the treetop. The beams intersected on a single trembling leaf, crimson as Mars, situated on a branch near the very top of the maple.

"There it is!" a little boy cried. "You see? There it is! That's the one!"

Sure enough, the leaf unchained itself from the limb that had been its home since spring. It fluttered toward the ground, swinging and swaying in the lilting breeze.

The town of Elderton applauded its descent.

Almo didn't stay to see the leaf alight upon the ground. Palm pressed against his lips, he started toward his home, still enveloped by the worry he'd expressed, still wondering how he and Elderton would save themselves from the looming invasion.

The crowd opened up to give the leaf space to land.

Land it did, and then quivered upon the ground, finally coming to rest where it would slowly lose its last shout of color, disintegrate, be caressed and absorbed by the earth beneath it.

Elderton's autumn had begun.

Chapter Five

Chandler Quinn leaned back in his recliner and puffed his pipe, then removed it from his mouth and pointed its stem toward the ceiling, tracing an oblique configuration in the air. Smoke curled from his lips, around his handlebar mustache, and wafted upward. "You know, Almo, death is like a period at the end of a sentence. Without a period, the sentence doesn't make sense. Without death, neither does life make sense. So you see, chum, apprehending the meaning of life and death is not a matter of religion or philosophy. It's a matter of syntax."

Chandler Quinn, Elderton's only practicing attorney (although he worked fewer than five hours per week), kept his long silver hair gathered in a ponytail, and his long handlebar mustache waxed at its tips. Tonight, as always, he wore a pinched expression on his face, as if the cardinal secret of life were skittering around the peripheries of his consciousness, just out of reach. He looked like an aging Jesus with a case of throbbing, itching hemorrhoids.

Almo straightened his small body on the davenport, paused, then said, "Don't you mean punctuation? I mean, you said a period is the important thing. That's punctuation, not syntax."

"Drat!" Chandler arced his arm through the air as if he were directing a symphony, then snapped his fingers. "You're right, of course. Well, there's another quotable quotation decimated into verbal dust."

"Why? Just substitute 'punctuation' for 'syntax' and you've got your quotation."

"No, sir," said Chandler, "it won't work. You know that. I have to formulate it properly the first time or it doesn't count. It must flow elegantly from brain to mouth. A personal rule."

"My goodness, Chandler, you've got a lot of rules for creativity."

Chandler shrugged. "A man must prescribe structure upon his existence, lest he live in a cloud of misty conceits."

Then, as quickly as the quotation had appeared and caressed his awareness, it disappeared completely from Chandler's mind. He arose from his chair and shuffled to the VCR. Hands on his knees, he peered thoughtfully at the blinking *12:00*.

"What's snatched your fancy now, Chandler?" Almo asked, leaning forward, elbows on knees.

"Another thought. It's not fully forgathered, so forgive me."

"You're forgiven."

"People—moments in time—are captured in magnetic particles that cling to and coat this videotape, am I right?"

"Yes, I suppose. Something like that."

"If there were some way to reverse the process, I could transfigure these particles back into a human being, could I not?"

"Hmm. Maybe."

"Well, sure I could. I'll need to ponder this a bit." Chandler wiped his mustache, twirled its tips. "Yes, I sense something substantial here."

Almo slid off the couch and waddled to Chandler's side. "Well, good luck with it, Chandler. I have to go home."

Chandler looked downward into Almo's eyes. "Understandable, chum. It *is* getting late. After one o'clock. But before you go . . ."

"Yes?"

"About what you proclaimed during the meeting to-night: our hallowed, hushed, poetic habitat contaminated by some external peril?"

"Something like that."

"This has to do with the crashed spacecraft?"

"I don't know for sure. I'd think so."

"How do you know?"

Almo smiled. "Silly question, Chandler. I don't know how I know, just like I don't know how I can predict the first falling autumn leaf or how you invent the things you invent or how any of Elderton's magic happens. I haven't a clue."

"So, an invasion, eh?" Chandler raised a finger into the air and directed his eyes to a cobwebbed corner of his ceiling. "Then I must immediately commence fashioning my . . . hmmm . . . Magnetic Particle Reversal Processor: MPRP, for short." An assured smile.

"Yeah? You think so?"

"Of course. If we're being invaded, we'll require succor. We've been peaceable for so long that if anything or anyone had a mind to assail us, we'd roll over like dead dogs."

"So how would your invention figure in?"

"Simple, chum. I'll reanimate a hero! That's what we need, isn't it? A hero."

Chapter Six

Ben held his fist an inch from the door, then stalled. It was six-thirty in the morning, after all. Should he be bothering Almo Parrish so early?

He shook his head, smiling. *What, am I getting soft? I'm a journalist, for Murrow's sake, and I'm on the trail of a potential fireball of a story. What the hell difference does it make? Besides, this is a farm town. People get up at the crack of dawn even when there isn't a lick of work to do, don't they?*

Yeah, screw him.

He rapped on the storm door three times. With his other hand he held up the shovel, so at least if the little Munchkin man peered through the window he would see that Ben had reason to be there so early. He'd come to return the shovel he'd borrowed, of course. Being a good neighbor, all that.

A scuffing sound from inside, then a bang, then a muffled bark of pain.

The door opened.

Almo Parrish stood there on one leg, hopping, his other leg bent upward behind him. He rubbed his foot. "Stubbed my toe," he said. The little bald man was clad in a tattered gray terrycloth bathrobe, his rim of hair sticking straight out like a tangle of hazel weeds.

"Sorry to bother you, Mr. Parrish," Ben said. "I just came to return your shovel."

He set down his leg and his eyes widened. "Oh, yes. Yes. You got that dog buried then?"

"Yes, the boy and I—"

"Jeffrey. Jeffrey Sprague. Good boy."

"Jeffrey. Yeah, he is. Well, we buried the dog, even held a little service of sorts."

"Good." A wink of approval.

Ben handed over the nice clean shovel.

Almo turned it over, inspecting the blade.

"I cleaned it up for you," Ben pointed out.

"I appreciate that."

Almo looked up, beagle-brown eyes focused on Ben's. "Well, I sure do appreciate you bringing back the shovel, young man."

Hearing the conversation coasting to a stop, Ben whipped out the only trump card in his possession, the only thing he thought might impress the man, keep him talking. "I used to live here, you know."

Almo's eyebrows raised. "You did?"

"Yeah, I was born here. My family moved when I was six. This is the first time I've been back."

Fists on hips, Almo said, "Well, I'll be a Jersey cow on a jet-ski. Born here, huh? A product of Elderton."

"That's right."

Ben heard Almo's voice warming up. Just what he wanted, needed. If there were a crashed UFO to be found here, he'd just made an important step toward jimmying important information. Almo Parrish had all the makings of a valuable source. He was known and respected by everyone in town, appearing to be the closest thing to an honorary mayor or ambassador that Elderton enjoyed. If anyone knew the truth, it was Almo Parrish.

Almo opened the front door wider. "Tell you what, son, why don't you come on inside. If you've got some time, I'll get myself ready and take you uptown for some coffee. How does that sound?"

All right! Success! I've nabbed me a Munchkin.

Stepping into the house, Ben smiled and said, "It sounds like the perfect antidote to a chilly fall morning."

Almo gestured toward the couch and Ben took a seat.

"You'll have to forgive me," Almo said. "I'm usually up and at 'em by five-thirty or so. Had a hard night last night."

"Trouble sleeping?"

"Something like that."

Almo excused himself and disappeared into the bathroom. As soon as Ben heard the sound of rushing water, he arose from the couch and scanned the contents of the living room. Nothing captured his attention at first. The general impression of the room was just short of dusty and unkempt. The furniture was tattered and probably had come from flea markets and garage sales. The wood trim was dull and unpolished, while the rug was crisscrossed by tiny bleached-out paths suggesting that Almo spent hours pacing it on his little feet. But the real curiosity was the absence of personal items, as though the occupier had taken a positive decision to have nothing around him that might remind him of his past.

Except for one thing. A picture. An eight-by-ten photograph sat atop the old black-and-white RCA television set, nestled within a tarnished brass frame.

Leaning over, Ben squinted his eyes to get a good look. There were familiar faces in the photo, including a few of the people who had been milling around after Ben hit the dog. A group of at least twenty people encircled Almo, who stood in front of the assembly, right arm draped over the shoulder of . . . Judy Garland?

What the hell?

Naaa. Couldn't be.

Sure, that boy Jeffrey had told Ben that Almo Parrish was the last surviving Munchkin from *The Wizard of Oz.*

But this picture was bogus. Had to be.

As bogus as Almo Parrish. Ben had known that the moment Jeffrey told him about the man. You just can't fool a city slicker journalist who has his foot dipped deeply into obscure popular culture.

One of Ben's first assignments after being hired at *The Astonished Eye* was to cover the grand opening of an Oz museum in northwestern Indiana. Several cast members had attended the gala event, all of them actors who had portrayed Munchkins in the movie, and who had come to leave their teeny handprints in the concrete surrounding a large flower garden. At the time, Ben (and his editor) had hoped that he would get the full, sordid story of the Munchkins' legendary sexual penchants. He hadn't succeeded—coming home with only a small item about how one Munchkin got drunk at the grand opening and gamely attempted to seduce a museum attendee dressed as the Wizard—but that was beside the point.

There were several Munchkins alive and, from what Ben knew, none of them was Almo Parrish. Sure, the Munchkins were getting up in years, but it simply wasn't possible that in the past six months they had *all* departed for that big lollipop heaven. Nope. Maybe Almo was a short humanoid, but no way was he a Munchkin. And hell, compared with most of the Munchkins, the guy wasn't even all that short.

The photograph only added fuel to Ben's incredulity. That was Judy Garland standing next to Almo, clear as day. A *cardboard cutout* of Judy Garland. Had to be. The sunlight reflected too harshly off the image.

"Like my picture?"

Startled, Ben stood up straight. "Yeah, very nice," he said, turning around and giving Almo his best smile. "When was it taken?"

"Oh, a few years ago," Almo said, scrubbing his dripping head with a large bath towel. "Pretty exciting."

What did Almo Parrish take Ben for? A consummate numskull? Judy Garland had been dead for years. And Almo expected Ben and everyone else who visited him to think that the dead actress made a special visit to Elderton to enjoy fellowship with her favorite fellow cast member? Sheesh. Apparently most of Almo's visitors found it easy to confuse cardboard with flesh.

"Let me throw on a shirt and coat and we can head for the coffee shop," Almo said, retreating into a bedroom at the end of the hallway.

He emerged a minute later and followed Ben to the Civic.

On their way to the town square, Ben cleared his throat. It was time to begin investigating in earnest, to take the first vital steps toward opening the can of extraterrestrial worms. "Hey, Almo, before I came back to visit my old hometown, I heard something strange."

"Yeah? What's that?"

Ben laughed, as though he thought what he was going to say was ridiculous. Well, he largely did. "It's apparently going around that a UFO—a craft from outer space—crashed near here."

"Well, isn't that somethin'." As noncommittal as a polygamist on his wedding day.

"Yeah. So I wonder what all of those people were talking about. Any ideas?"

"Ideas? I have a few."

"Tell me. I'm a writer, you see—a *journalist*—and I like to track urban legends: you know, stories with charm but no validity that get passed around, like the hook-armed man who spooks the kids while they're making out on Lovers'

Lane, or pushers getting kids hooked on drugs with LSD-laced Mickey Mouse tattoos, or the Doberman who coughs up a burglar's fingers when his owners return home. That kind of thing."

"I know what you mean. Say, what paper did you say you work for?"

"Uh, *The Astonished Eye.*"

"Hmm, never heard of it. Did they take the name from the Kenneth Patchen poem?"

"Well, gosh, I don't know." Ben had always assumed that the title of the paper was just something dreamed up to go with the logo of the bulging, bloodshot eye on the masthead.

"Makes you wonder," said Almo.

"So, any ideas about this story?"

"The best idea I have is this," Almo said, folding his hands in his lap. "Maybe it happened."

"Maybe it happened?"

"Sure. Perhaps you don't remember so well, but this is Elderton, Illinois, my friend. Unusual things happen around here all the time. It's our little blessing, I guess you'd say. If one of those spaceships was going to come down, it wouldn't surprise me one little bit if it landed near Elderton."

"Fascinating," Ben said. He tried to extinguish the flame of excitement that had begun lapping at the center of his chest. "Gosh, so you think it might just be true, huh?"

"I'd almost bet on it." Almo nodded absently, then said nothing more.

Ben wanted to continue. So close. But he decided against it. Obviously Almo was being guarded, testing the waters with Ben. Better to earn a little more trust before squeezing the facts out of the Munchkin.

Good Lord, what if there is *a crashed UFO near here? Could it be?* Ben briefly pictured himself being interviewed by network anchors and talk show hosts. Nice.

Ben drove onto the town square, impressed with the stately courthouse, as well as the stores facing it from all four sides. Each was built of brick—many of them sporting cornerstones from the 1800s—and so clean and bright they must have been sandblasted not too long ago. He also noticed how each building housed an active, open store. When he'd traveled through downstate Illinois, most of the small towns' business districts had been annihilated by the arrival of Wal-Mart and the other superstores. Here, the small mom-and-pop stores were still open for business, appearing well cared for and prosperous. Proudly incongruous with much of downstate Illinois.

They stopped at Duane and Joyce's Coffee Shop on the north side of the square. Like all of the businesses, it possessed a 1950s charm. An awning with blue and white stripes shaded its entrance, and shiny Formica-covered tables were scattered across the small shop, many of them rearranged and pushed together into friendly configurations to meet the social needs of the locals.

Almo and Ben entered amidst the clatter of dishes and the muted murmurs of at least twenty voices sharing gossip and weather editorials.

They took a table in the corner and, after Almo had politely introduced Ben to their waitress Maggie (and several other Eldertonians within earshot), they ordered coffee.

As Maggie set down the cups in front of them, Ben said to Almo, "Boy, it's nice to be back here. It feels like home already." Lying.

"Happy you feel that way," Almo said, smiling. "What's your most treasured memory from your years here?"

That stopped Ben in his verbal tracks. He'd been here nearly a day and had yet to remember one thing from the time his family had lived in Elderton. Not one person, one building, one situation. Not one scintilla of data upon which to hang his conversational hat.

Nothing.

"Gosh, there's so much," Ben lied again, and then searched his mind for a positive yet vague assessment. "I guess what I remember most is just the sense of peace and cooperation around town. Compassion."

"Compassion," Almo said. "You know, my friend Chandler Quinn has a little formula that he claims mathematically describes compassion."

"What's that?"

"Compassion equals pity minus condescension."

"I like that." Actually, it wasn't bad. Maybe someday Ben could use that line in a story.

Right. As if he ever worked a story involving compassion.

"Yeah," Almo said. "I like it, too."

"Say," Ben said, "I just had a funny thought. Do you think there's anybody in here who could help me with this UFO story?"

Almo swept his head around, surveying the chattering patrons. "Nope," he said. "No one here fits that description."

"I see."

Ben turned and looked around the coffee shop. Everyone was involved in his or her own little conclave. Even more amazing, all of them were smiling and enjoying themselves. It was almost spooky. In Chicago, he couldn't get a cup of cappuccino without encountering at least a handful of bubble-eyed shriekers.

As Almo and Ben sat drinking their coffee, several people came up to their table, giving Almo a hearty good morning and a pat on the shoulder. Three of them even greeted Ben by name, welcoming him home. He wanted to ask them details about his forgotten life but quickly reconsidered, deciding it was best not to display total ignorance of his personal history.

Abruptly, Ben's attention was seized by a figure just outside the big picture window facing the spacious courtyard. A little girl was walking along the sidewalk; stumbling, really—her eyes dull marbles, her dark hair mussed, mud smudged and caked across the front of her frilly pink dress.

"Look at that," Ben said, touching Almo's wrist. "There's something the matter with that girl."

Almo calmly blew across his coffee's surface, then took a sip. He shook his head. "It's all right," he said, peering intently at his coffee. "That's Vida Proust."

"But look at her," Ben said, pointing again before the girl lumbered out of view.

"Vida hasn't been feeling well for a couple of weeks. Don't worry about her. We're keeping an eye on her. We'll take care of her. We take care of our own around here."

Good Lord. I've stumbled into some kind of lunatic colony. Even if there weren't a UFO story to sniff out here, I've seen enough to write at least four good stories for the paper.

PSYCHOTIC PARADISE FOUND HIDDEN IN RURAL ILLINOIS

Yes, that could be the big story. But there are so many other possibilities:

DIRTY, ABUSED GIRL ALLOWED TO WANDER AIMLESSLY, IGNORED BY SMALL TOWN

BLIND VOYEUR TERRORIZES TINY VILLAGE

DELUSIONAL MIDGET BELIEVES HE STARRED
IN FAMOUS MOVIE, POSES WITH
CARDBOARD CUTOUT

"Yep, it's sure nice to be home," Ben said, then took a big swig of his coffee.

Chapter Seven

She had been following him for three blocks, ever since Jeffrey left the First Methodist Church of Elderton, where he'd slept last night.

At first the sight of the dirty little girl—walking kind of like the Frankenstein monster: arms stiff, locked legs unsteady—sent a tremor snaking up his spine.

He walked faster.

It didn't seem to matter how quickly he walked. Every time he looked behind him, she was there.

He stopped and pondered the situation. So many times people had shunned him without even getting to know him, because he looked or acted a little different or because he didn't seem to belong anywhere. But his arrival in Elderton offered a chance to alter that legacy, it seemed, and if he were going to change his role in this sorry world, perhaps this was the perfect opportunity.

So he turned around and waited.

Although she looked to be struggling painfully every step of the way, when she finally was toe-to-toe with Jeffrey she wasn't even breathing hard. She was as placid as a winter pond, and almost as white.

He felt a sudden urge to do something his mother had always done when she was alive: to lick his fingers and scrub the smudges off the little girl's face, or brush off the front of her dress. He restrained himself. He didn't even know this girl.

For several swollen moments, they stood there—toes to toes, eyes to eyes—neither saying a word.

Finally Jeffrey punctured the silence. "Uh, hi."

The muscles of her face were slack, as if they'd been hastily glued to her skull. They barely moved when she said, "Hello." Her voice was flat, and too husky for a little girl no older than Jeffrey.

She touched him on the arm.

So cold.

"Are you okay?" Jeffrey asked.

"Where did you sleep last night?" the little girl said, as if she hadn't heard Jeffrey's question.

"The church. It's unlocked. Took a spit bath in there, then went to sleep under a pew. I found a plate of eggs and bacon and a glass of milk outside this morning, so I even ate."

The very edges of her lips turned up, a faint smile. "Good. You're rested then. And full."

"Yes, I am."

"Do you want to walk me to school?"

Jeffrey paused. This morning when he'd awakened, one of the first things he'd thought about was that he ought to find the local school and enroll. Maybe he could make up something about where he lived, and with whom. It would be a step toward taking responsibility for himself. Other than running away from foster homes and skipping school, this was something he had had neither the occasion nor the inclination to do since Mom died.

"Well, sure," Jeffrey answered, smiling faintly himself now.

She turned stiffly and began walking. Jeffrey followed her.

Once he was alongside her, the little girl slipped her left arm around his right arm.

So cold.

Jeffrey decided to try again. "Are you sure you're okay? You don't look well. Are you sick or something?"

"I feel okay. I need to get to school."

Finally. A response.

"Good," Jeffrey said, proud to have made contact with this lonely, dirty little girl. "I need to get to school, too. I'm happy you found me. My name's Jeffrey. Jeffrey Sprague."

"My name is Vida Proust," the little girl responded. Then, out of nowhere she added, "You miss your dog."

"How did you know about that?"

The little girl remained silent.

"Well, I *do* miss my dog," Jeffrey said. "He was a good boy. Found him out in the forest. He was wearing a sweater. He kind of adopted me, and I adopted him back. He helped me find my way here."

"It's too bad he's been buried," she said. "You could still be playing with him or hugging him or teaching him tricks."

Jeffrey had no idea how to respond to that, so he kept his mouth shut.

Straight ahead, a red brick schoolhouse, square and three stories tall, came into view.

"Is that where we go to school?" Jeffrey asked.

"It is," answered the girl.

Arms still interlocked, they walked up the concrete steps of the school and found themselves amid a flock of junior high students milling around the hallway.

"Hiya, Vida," a boy said as he passed. "You sure look good today."

"Vida," a girl said, "who's your friend?"

Vida turned her head jerkily and answered, "Jeffrey Sprague."

"Is he coming to school here?" the girl asked.

65

"Yes," Vida said, jerking her head back, again facing straight ahead.

Vida led Jeffrey into a classroom.

"Where do I sit?" Jeffrey said, feeling almost overwhelmed by how effortlessly everything was happening. "Don't I need to check in with the office or something, tell them I'm here?"

"You can sit with me," Vida said, now taking him by the arm with her icy hand and guiding him to the back of the room. Two straight-backed oaken chairs sat against the back wall. Releasing Jeffrey's arm, Vida sat down. Jeffrey took the seat beside her.

During the next ten minutes, the classroom filled with students, many of them nodding to Vida, or coming up and introducing themselves to Jeffrey. He remembered back to all of the schools he'd attended. This had never happened before.

He was so happy he'd found Vida. So happy he'd come. Already Jeffrey felt almost at home, like he actually belonged here. It was a chance, perhaps his last, to find a new role for himself. He could be the real Jeffrey Sprague for a change. If only he could remember who he'd once been.

A little after eight, a shrill bell rang, echoing down the hallway.

The teacher walked in. Jeffrey's breath moored in his throat.

She was so beautiful. Her hair was blond, cut short, and her eyes were the precise color of a clear summer sky. Her sleek body moved lithely around the room. As she spoke in her soft and rhythmic voice, she gracefully moved her arms, which were thin and as delicate looking as china. Her long fingernails were painted a warm red.

And for some reason, what Jeffrey noticed most of all was her neck. It looked strong and noble.

This was a boy who never had bonded with any of the foster families with whom he'd lived, much less teachers or classmates. Yet here he was, feeling the warm sensations of a schoolboy crush the moment he set eyes on his new teacher. God, it felt good.

"Good morning, class," the teacher said, smiling widely, thin eyebrows arched expectantly.

In unison, the students said, almost sang, "Good morning, Miss Gayle."

"I understand we have a new student today," she said, looking straight at Jeffrey.

He thought his heart would melt right then and there. He was simultaneously stunned that word of his arrival had spread so quickly, and warmly overwhelmed with the mere awareness that this beautiful woman was noticing him.

Again in unison, each classmate's head turned around to look at Jeffrey.

He gave a little, tentative wave.

"What's your name, young man?" the beautiful teacher asked.

"Jeffrey Sprague."

"Class, let's all welcome Jeffrey."

Singing: "Welcome, Jeffrey."

Miss Gayle said, "Vida, were you nice enough to bring Jeffrey with you today?"

"Yes I was," Vida said in her flat, husky voice.

"Aren't you a wonderful hostess," Miss Gayle said, smile spreading even wider as she winked.

During the next two hours, Jeffrey sat entranced as Miss Gayle talked about American history, showed the students how to do math problems, and arranged them in groups to draw pictures.

Jeffrey drew a picture of Miss Gayle, or at least he tried

to. There was no way he could capture even a shred of her beauty. When she walked past, he covered the pencil sketch with his arms and felt his face burning.

Time flew. Before he knew it, the harsh bell rang, signaling recess.

Jeffrey merged with the mass of students leaving the classroom. Just as he neared the doorway, Miss Gayle came up behind him and touched him on the back. Her touch was as warm as Vida's was cold.

"I just want to tell you how happy I am you're joining our class, Jeffrey."

He opened his dry mouth, but the first thing that came out was a hoarse little crack. He cleared his throat, then said, "Thank you, ma'am. Do I need to go to the office or something?"

"For heaven's sake, why?"

"I don't know. To sign up or something."

Miss Gayle smiled, shook her head. "Don't you worry about that, Jeffrey. We'll take care of everything for you."

Nodding, head swimming with happiness, Jeffrey left the room and walked into the hallway.

He couldn't see Vida anywhere, but that was okay. He didn't feel a bit threatened or nervous. He'd find things by himself and—who knew—he might even meet some more people, make a friend or two.

Following the flock of students, he nodded and smiled at everyone who made eye contact with him. He hadn't felt this good since months before Mom died.

He felt a tug on his right shoulder, turned, and faced a large boy standing there. For some reason, Jeffrey immediately knew that this boy wasn't like the rest of the students he'd seen. He looked rough around the edges, overweight, even a little angry.

"You the new kid?"

"Yeah," Jeffrey answered.

"How'd you get here?"

Jeffrey had yet to get a feel for this boy's intents and decided not to volunteer any more information than was required. "I walked here with Vida Proust."

"Vida, huh? So do you like her, kid?"

Jeffrey frowned. "Well, I'm not in love with her or anything, but she seems nice and all."

The boy shook his head. "*I'm* gonna be your friend, kid, and tell you a couple things. First off, you got treated pretty good when you got here, didn't you?"

"Yes, I did."

"Well, enjoy it while you can. Sure, they'll be nice to you as long as you're coming. But if you try to leave or skip school or something . . . watch out. They'll do something to you." The boy smirked.

"Why? What'll they do?"

"I'm not sure, and even if I was, I wouldn't tell you. But I will tell you something else that'll prove you haven't just stumbled into heaven or something."

"What's that?"

"Vida? That girl who brought you to school?"

"Yeah?"

The kid's eyes nervously darted left to right. Then he bent close to Jeffrey's ear and whispered, "She's been dead for three weeks."

Chapter Eight

"How in heaven's name did you put that thing together?" Hands behind his back, Almo leaned forward, squinting his eyes as he struggled to identify the components making up the piano-sized contraption Chandler had assembled in his living room.

A few of them were familiar: the staple gun; the old Philco console radio; the husk of a refrigerator; the series of horseshoe magnets bound together with endless strings of blinking Christmas lights; two bicycle wheels; a storm window; and tendrils of orange extension cords that wound around and around the entire chaotic display. But most of it was impossible to identify, just a tangled aggregation of gears and wires and switches.

Sleeves pushed up, scratching his forehead with a socket wrench, Chandler stepped back to admire his handiwork. "Of course you know the answer to that, my friend. I possess nary an intimation. When I wakened this morning I was suddenly seized by what I can only describe as unearthly inspiration; I could visualize the device so trenchantly. It's taken me only two hours to fabricate it. Before long it shall be a functional gestalt, prepared for operation."

"And so this is your . . . what did you call it?"

"My Magnetic Particle Reversal Processor: MPRP, for short."

"And with this, you plan to reanimate someone from a videotape?"

"Most certainly," Chandler said, eyebrows wriggling like hairy caterpillars, and smiling as if he were stating a simple fact of life. "Can't you see it's hooked up to my video-cassette recorder? See that one wire?"

"Well, sure."

Chandler wiped his hand across his eyes, let his shoulders slump, and sighed. "My goodness, my ageless friend, this frenzy of creativity has suddenly left me bereft of vigor. I require respite."

"Good. I was hoping you'd say that. Is your car in working order?"

"Well, it hasn't been running all that well. I can't seem to repair it."

"Will it get us, let's say, a few miles?"

"But of course!"

"Let's take a ride then. I need to talk to you about a serious decision I'm facing, and I need to show you something."

"What do you want to show me?"

Almo paused briefly. "Well, *I* woke up this morning with a clear view of where the spacecraft crashed."

"Wonderful!" Chandler exclaimed. "Perhaps we'll have no need for my MPRP after all. Perhaps we can anticipate, then locate, then eradicate the interloper."

Suddenly, Almo looked crestfallen. "Perhaps. *If* it is the invader."

"Why the long face, my short friend?"

"I don't know yet."

"Magma in the stomach? Cannonade in the head?"

"Something like that."

They left Chandler's house and secured themselves in his old fungus-colored Rambler, which reeked of pipe smoke and scorched oil. Chandler turned the key and the squat beast coughed itself to life.

"Aha!" Chandler said, smiling proudly. "A rare and welcome exception: engaging on the initial attempt. You know something, Almo? Of all the flair I possess for tinkering with things mechanical, this particular phaeton consistently thwarts me like a screen window curses a winter fly."

Almo didn't respond.

"Are you sure you're okay, my friend?" Chandler asked as he backed out of the driveway.

"I don't know."

"Go on, then. Spill it like mercury from a paper cup. Out with it. This is Chandler Quinn you're talking to."

Chandler drove around the square before heading south, toward Lou Bentley's farm some two miles beyond the city limits.

When Almo still hadn't responded, Chandler ventured a guess. "It's that visitor, isn't it?"

"Ben Savitch, right."

"What's the matter then? I sensed your initial impression was laudatory."

"Well, it is. I mean, he's a hometown boy, even though he hasn't lived here in decades."

"Almo, you're the heart of this town, you know that. Why not trust your instincts?"

"I don't know. I'd sure like to share everything we know, everything we have, with him. Being born here, it seems like he deserves it. And he might be the person who can help us. Still . . ."

" 'Still' what?"

"Every time I think of doing that, there's a shudder up my spine like you wouldn't believe."

Chandler took a left onto a dirt lane.

"Mm-hmm," said Chandler thoughtfully. "So in other words, your heart and your spinal column are at odds with one another."

"Something like that."

"My friend, perhaps you should struggle with the question you pose to us so regularly."

"What's that?"

"You're on the deck of the Titanic. What do you want to do now?"

Chandler steered the Rambler through an open gate in the barbed wire fence, entering a long, sweeping pasture lush with all forms of tall, swaying prairie grass: Feather Reed, Frost Grass, Purple Moor, Blue Lyme.

"Well, we now inhabit Lou Bentley's private property," Chandler said. "Everyone knows the craft plummeted to earth near here, but no one's been out to see it. We've been waiting for you to take the first look and tender your astute assessment. So Almo, point the way, my internally conflicted human friend."

Still distracted by thoughts, Almo nonetheless pointed a stubby finger westward, without even looking.

"Good enough," said Chandler, turning the Rambler and heading that direction. The old car squeaked in protest as it swayed and lurched its way over bumps and through ruts in the luscious pasture.

"Well, take my cranium and fashion a soup bowl out of it." Instinctively, Chandler removed his pipe from his front pocket and jammed it between his teeth. It began vibrating, quaking up and down in a near-blur with his escalating excitement.

They had just driven over the crest of a long, sloping hill and now were looking down into a half-dry creek bed. There lay what was the most curious object either of them had ever seen. It was the alien spacecraft, had to be. But it wasn't a saucer-shaped metallic object, nothing like that. It was smaller than a Volkswagen Bug and shaped like a teardrop or a crystalline Christmas ornament. Rather than being made of shiny metal or steel, the craft was oddly translucent, shimmering in the bright autumn sunlight as if it were sculpted from the skin of a jellyfish.

Chandler stopped the car, shoved the gearshift into Park, and engaged the emergency brake. Having had the car start so easily, he wasn't going to tempt fate. He would leave it running.

Almo and Chandler exited the car, exchanging neither words nor glances as they walked side by side down the gentle incline. The nearer they got to the UFO, the thicker the beautiful prairie grass became. It gave off a potent, achingly sweet scent. As they walked, the dense mass of prairie grass bent almost politely to let the two pass, then again stood upright.

Arriving at the craft, Chandler took the pipe out of his mouth and gently poked the craft with its stem, then gingerly rubbed it with his index finger. "It's almost silken," he said in a reverent whisper.

"Look over here," said Almo, pointing, "there's an opening on this side."

They sloshed through the shallow, cold creek water. Sure enough, there was a rupture, no larger than a dinner plate, on the side of the craft.

Almo leaned close and peered inside. "No one here. Just a seat of some kind. I don't see any controls, not even a steering wheel."

"Then our invader is now an evacuee," Chandler said decisively. "Shall we ferret it out?"

Almo knelt and ran his hand across the creek's muddy bank. "There *are* a few footprints here. Little ones."

"Then by all means, my investigative cohort, let us pursue the entity from beyond!"

Chapter Nine

"You don't believe me, Jeffrey," said Bert Frehley, the kid who had shared the unnerving information about Vida Proust. "I can tell by the look on your face." He rested his fists on his ample hips, waiting for a response.

They stood in front of the schoolhouse, where Bert had been waiting for him. At first, Jeffrey had wondered whether the boy was a closet bully after all and wanted to put the newcomer in his place by thumping him on the noggin a few times. But no, now Bert seemed subtly upset, not threatening at all.

Jeffrey continued looking around the playground. He hadn't seen Vida for the remainder of the day. He had asked Miss Gayle about her as the last bell sounded, and Miss Gayle had smiled her beautiful smile and said that Vida had gone home sick, that she was sure the little girl would be okay by tomorrow.

"I just don't know what I should believe," Jeffrey said. "I mean, you said she was dead. If she was dead, how come she was walking around?"

Bert shrugged, wrinkling his forehead into a question mark. "Beats me. I don't know why a lot of things happen around here. Did you see it when everybody met on the square last night?"

"Well, I saw a crowd but that's when I was looking for a place to sleep, so I didn't follow them or anything. I heard them clapping."

"Well, let me tell you: they were meeting because every year, Almo Parrish points out the first autumn leaf that's gonna fall."

"How does he do that?"

"You're askin' too many questions, kid. I don't have any idea, that's the point! But I was there. I saw it happen."

"So you're saying that this town is haunted or magic or what?"

"One of those. Maybe something else, something worse. All I know for sure is that I ran away from home six weeks ago—"

"*You* ran away?"

"You bet. Walked all the way here from Quincy. My Dad beat me up all the time."

"Sorry."

"And ever since I got here, people have been treating me like I was the nicest kid you'd ever want to meet, a little prince or something. They even gave me a home to stay in."

"A home? Where do you live?"

"With Miss Gayle."

A horn honked. Both boys turned.

Miss Gayle pulled up to the curb in a shiny rose-colored Toyota Camry. She rolled down her window. "You boys need a ride?"

Jeffrey felt that dry crack in his throat again. He couldn't speak.

Bert smiled a winning, fake smile. "Sure, Miss Gayle." He started for the car.

Jeffrey was frozen in place. He couldn't tell whether it was uncertainty that had affixed him to the ground, or the warmhearted enchantment he felt whenever he saw Miss Gayle's face.

Bert got into the front seat of the car.

Still looking straight into Jeffrey's eyes, the schoolteacher asked, "Are you coming, Jeffrey Sprague?"

"Uh, sure, I guess."

Suddenly unshackled, he skipped to the car and piled into the back seat, immediately being enveloped by the soothing smell of Miss Gayle's heavenly perfume. He took a deep breath, slumped in his seat and let it intoxicate him.

She drove to her home, a split-level brick house sitting in a small, tidy subdivision at the northernmost edge of town.

Turning off the engine, she said, "Do you need to go get anything, Jeffrey? Any clothes?"

"No. I don't have any."

She laughed. "That's no problem. I'm sure we can fix you right up. Right, Bert?"

"Right, Miss Gayle," Bert said like a robot, without missing a beat.

She led the two boys inside.

The house smelled so clean, and its decor was tasteful, neatly arranged. Everything from the overstuffed armchair to the couch to the wallpaper was decorated with patterns of light blue flowers. Everything from the kitchen table to the cabinets to the upright piano shined so brightly he imagined he could part his hair by looking into them.

Jeffrey had never seen a home so . . . well, so perfect.

"C'mon, Jeffrey," Bert said, slapping Jeffrey on the back. "I'll show you our room."

"Wonderful," said Miss Gayle. "You boys go in there and get comfortable. I'll call you when dinner's ready."

Bert led Jeffrey to a bedroom at the rear of the house. A large window looked out upon a tree resplendent with colorful autumn leaves. Two school desks were situated in opposite corners. Two oaken chests-of-drawers sat side by side; one of them had its empty drawers pulled half open. Most surprising of all, there were two double beds in the room.

Almost as if Jeffrey had been expected.

Bert took a short run and leapt upon a bed. "The other

one's yours," he said, lying back with his head on the pillow, fingers interlocked behind his neck.

Jeffrey sat down on the other bed. He patted it twice, then rubbed his hand across the soft bedspread, still trying to get accustomed to the idea that he had a bed of his own, in a clean warm house where the most beautiful woman in the world lived.

He slipped off his shoes, then swung his legs up on the bed and lay down, duplicating Bert's position.

"This is something, isn't it?" Bert asked.

"Sure is."

"And that makes what I'm gonna do seem that much weirder, I know."

"What are you going to do?"

"Run away."

Jeffrey sat up straight and shot Bert a confused glance. "Run away? Why?"

Bert shook his head and sighed. "There's just something not right here. At least with my Dad, I know what's coming when I see the look on his face. Here, I don't know what's gonna happen next."

Jeffrey couldn't think of a thing to say. He had only been here a few minutes, but already he was feeling at home. Safe. Secure. So comfortable it almost scared him. Maybe that was it. "You're just not used to being treated so good? Could that be it?"

Bert let out a low laugh. "Didn't you hear what I was telling you earlier? About Vida Proust? The little dead girl?"

"Well, yeah, but I can't say I beli—"

"Listen, kid, I saw them drag her body out of a well. She'd been out playing and fell in. She was dead. I ain't seen anyone dead before but she was dead. Believe me on that."

Jeffrey frowned. Bert seemed a bit unhinged. "Then how's she walking around?"

Bert laughed again. "Hope. Politeness. Sorcery. Black magic. Heck, I don't know."

"Huh?"

"The way I understand it, maybe she doesn't realize she's dead. And the town's too polite to tell her. A bunch of people—kids *and* grown-ups—came up to me after I saw her dead, and told me not to tell her. It's like they hoped her back alive or something. Her parents were there and they were really upset."

"Why wouldn't they be?"

"No, man, not because she was dead. Because they said she'd been dead too long. They said the town should just let her rest but the other people wouldn't hear of it. They brought her back anyway."

"That's crazy."

"Now you're gettin' the point."

"But even if that stuff about Vida is true, how's that hurting you? Why would you want to run away?"

"They got something planned for us, for all the kids in town. I guess it's something they do every year, after the first leaf falls. Some of the kids at school were telling me."

"What's that?"

"They blindfold us and take us out into the country, to this secret place they call the Presence Chamber."

"What happens there?"

"I don't have any idea," Bert said. "That's what's got me scared."

Chapter Ten

Standing on the crest of a hill, Ben lowered the binoculars from his eyes.

"Bingo," he said to himself, letting the word be carried away by the aromatic September wind. "Bingo-reeno."

He'd been staking out Chandler Quinn's house ever since dropping off Almo there. The course of the coffee shop conversation he'd had with Almo told him that just beneath the surface of the diminutive fraud was a footlocker full of secrets. After Chandler Quinn had walked into the coffee shop and Almo seemed so nervously intent that they meet soon, Ben knew without a doubt that something was up.

He'd parked a block away. Then, when the two emerged from the house, he trailed Chandler Quinn's chugging Rambler at a safe distance, ending up here at the immense expanse of beautiful pastureland on Lou Bentley's property.

Raising the binoculars back to his eyes, he once again zeroed in on the small crashed spacecraft, excitement churning inside him. Then he focused the binoculars with his index fingers and trained his view on Almo and Chandler, who were scrambling up the side of a far hill, heads bent toward the ground like bipedal bloodhounds.

They're on the trail of the alien. That has to be it.

After the two disappeared over the rise, Ben tossed the binoculars through the open window of his car, then leapt over the barbed wire fence separating him from the pasture, from the crashed UFO, from his future of fame and celebrity and meaning.

Tugged along by gravity and anticipation, he nearly fell three times as he barreled down the hill, slipping and sliding, not totally out of control but certainly never in control. Finally he did lose his balance but even that felt wonderful, almost graceful. He fell face forward, did a complete somersault through the caresses of the prairie grass, then slid on his butt the rest of the way down, until the soles of his shoes were mere inches from the craft.

He was mesmerized by its foreign translucence, almost fearful to touch it lest he be drawn into its crystalline beauty. But slowly, he did reach out and graze its side with his right palm. It felt like it was covered with airy velvet, so soft it made him want to smile or weep.

Observing the small hole gouged in the far side of the small craft, Ben jumped over the narrow creek to the other bank. He reached out and grabbed hold of a tattered edge of the breach in its hull, then began working the impossibly soft material back and forth.

"Evidence," he said aloud, already fantasizing about calling up his college buddy Max Thomason and boasting about his find until Max collapsed into a trembling, envious heap. "Evidence."

Fingers clutched Ben's right shoulder. Painfully.

Ben released his hold on the craft and pitched backward, breath anchoring in his throat. He turned around quickly, prepared to raise his fists to anyone who might steal this moment from him.

The tall blind man from the motel window stood there, wearing the same overalls, the same dreadful smile, still moving his lips and mouthing unknown words.

Before Ben had a chance to protest, the blind man yanked him to his feet, then pulled him close until they were nearly nose to nose. A shiver traveled through Ben's body as he looked into the milky, wandering eyes.

The man kept mouthing words, lips wriggling like little worms.

"What?" Ben said, hearing his voice as weak as it had ever been. "What do you want?"

The blind man leaned closer. Ben had to turn his head to avoid vomiting from the rotten-teeth odor of the man's breath.

Beginning to gather his wits, Ben looked back at the blind man and stared intently at his mouth. Perhaps if he could just understand what the man was trying to say, he could figure this all out, get rid of the creep, and resume collecting the evidence he needed to write the greatest story of his career.

It took nearly a minute, but by listening to the man's voiceless words being shaped in the air, he finally understood.

Lead me, the blind man was mouthing. *Lead me.*

"Where?" Ben said. "Lead you where?"

The blind man gave his head a little jerk, and Ben followed the gesture. He was indicating the top of the hill, where Ben's car sat, barely visible over the rise.

Ben tried to think quickly. The blind man wanted a ride, it seemed. Okay. He could take the blind man wherever he wanted to go, drop him off, then rush back here. As long as the UFO had sat here undisturbed, it wasn't like anyone was going to come out and carry it off while he was gone. The trip wouldn't take more than ten minutes. Better that then getting into a bloody brawl with a blind man. Always the pragmatist, Ben was.

But he was marshaling some strength now, and another part of Ben—the part that had wandered the streets of downtown Chicago and learned to fend for itself—vetoed such a neighborly approach. No, instead he would do what he'd done a hundred times when eluding blind beggars in the Loop. He'd sneak off. The guy *was* blind, after all.

As if he'd read Ben's intent and was happy to cooperate, the man relaxed his grip on Ben's shoulders.

Ben pulled away, jumped over the creek, and ran faster than he'd run since being caught with the editor's wife when he was working for *Signal News* in Akron.

He made it halfway up the hill when the wet soles of his shoes betrayed him. He slipped and fell on his face.

That's okay, Ben thought, fingers clamped around the damp grass, nose pressed against the ground. *Just lie still. The guy can't see.* He pinched his lips together, quieting his breath. For nearly a minute, he didn't move a muscle.

Then, slowly, Ben turned his head.

The blind man stood above him, motionless, that horrid smile on his face, the smile filled with rotten teeth and far too many empty spaces.

Making as little sound as possible, Ben stood up and faced the blind man.

The man didn't move, still smiling, eyes meandering between heaven and earth.

Straining every muscle in his body, Ben suddenly took three leaping backward steps up the hill.

The blind man did the same. Three steps.

Ben took four backward steps. The blind man followed. Exactly. As if he could portend every move Ben was going to make.

Ben ran to his left. The blind man followed.

He wasn't going to fool this one, despite all of the practice he'd had throughout his childhood.

Only one thing left to do. Run like hell.

Ben turned, leaned down until his fists were pressed against the ground, then began scrambling up the hillside.

He made it five steps when the blind man leapt onto his back and rode him to the earth.

Ben lay flat on his face, the blind man on his back.

He felt the blind man shift his weight, moving up Ben's body until his lips touched Ben's ear.

"Lead me," he whispered.

Chapter Eleven

"May I have some more milk?" Jeffrey asked. Crumbs from a freshly consumed brownie were strewn across his lips.

Audrey Gayle smiled. "Well, of course," she said, getting up from the table.

As she opened the refrigerator door, she asked, "So, how do you like it here so far, Jeffrey?"

He wiped his forearm across his mouth. "I like it just fine, thank you."

A great, warm wave flowed through Audrey. When she'd returned to Elderton two months ago to teach, she'd wanted only to give back to the community a little of the concern she had been shown while growing up here, to share the meaningful magic that had been central to her childhood. But Elderton's promise now seemed so much stronger than she'd anticipated.

Leaving town after high school, Audrey had attended college at the University of Illinois, then spent nearly twenty years teaching in various school districts across the Midwest. While she'd loved every school year, every student, her life never seemed complete or settled.

One day, while her seventh graders in Bloomington took an algebra test, it had struck her: while she'd learned how to fly and soar, she had yet to make a nest, a soft cradle of belongingness that would make her nights and weekends as full and meaningful as her days. She had been meeting the needs of youngsters so consistently over the years, but somewhere in the process she had forgotten herself. And she knew deep inside that the best place for her to build a nest was Elderton.

She was so happy she'd made the decision to return, happier still to learn that her own seventh grade teacher, Mrs. Daly, had retired just in time for Audrey's return. Tonight, it seemed like everything was falling into place, or at the very least showing inspiring potential.

There couldn't have been a more welcome addition to her household than Jeffrey Sprague. Looking into his innocent blue eyes, she could see all the joyful promise residing within the boy, nestled beneath a mountain of dashed hopes. A few weeks here and that mountain would crumble into dust. She knew it. She had faith that Elderton would heal Jeffrey Sprague.

Bert was another story. He worried Audrey. Even now, as he sat ostensibly content at the kitchen table, his unease was palpable. She hoped she would be able to reach him, that Elderton would reach him.

She poured Jeffrey's milk and had just sat down again when the phone rang.

"Audrey?"

"Yes?"

"It's Almo."

"Oh, hi, Almo." She felt the smile that graced her face every time she heard the last Munchkin's voice. Almo had been the first to greet her upon her return to Elderton and had become a frequent visitor, a touchstone for all the things her hometown represented.

"Things are coming together," he said, though it was unclear whether that was good or bad.

"I see," she said, hoping he'd explain.

"As I said at the courtyard last night, we're going to be invaded."

"I know," she said. "Any clearer idea of what's going to happen?"

The last Munchkin paused for a second before saying, "Not really, no. But the feeling inside me, it's so horrible. Right now, it seems to me that the best thing we can do is fortify the bonds among all of us. We're on the deck of the Titanic and I, for one, think we should hold on tight to one another for support. Share the lifeboat."

"I understand. So that means . . . ?"

"That means that those two boys who are living with you need to become part of Elderton. We need everyone. You never know where our strength is going to come from. It could well be within one of those two youngsters. So how about if I have someone pick them up tonight—say about nine—and take them out to the Presence Chamber?"

Audrey checked her watch. Six-thirty. "That won't be a problem, Almo. I'll have a little talk with them, and they'll be ready at eight."

"Bless your heart, Audrey. Goodbye."

She hung up the phone and returned to the table, where Jeffrey sat finishing off the last of his milk and Bert was staring at her, a hint of fear clouding his eyes.

"Boys, you're going to be taking a little trip tonight."

She saw the alarm in Bert's eyes redoubling so she quickly added, with a smile, "A short little trip. It'll be fun, I promise. And you'll be home in time to take a bath and finish your homework."

"Okay," Jeffrey responded, smiling back.

Bert nodded.

Out of nowhere, Jeffrey pressed his lips together for a moment, then let the words fly as if they'd been bottled up for a week: "I really like it here, Miss Gayle. Elderton seems like such a nice place and you're, well, you're about the nicest person I've ever met in my whole life . . . besides my parents, I mean." He looked down at the table, face burning red.

"Awww. That's sweet of you to say, Jeffrey."

"And I'll go anywhere you think I should go," he added. "I'll do anything you want."

She reached over and patted his forearm. "You're a real gentleman, do you know that?"

"What's gonna happen tonight?" Bert said suddenly, staccato words.

Audrey patted her mouth with the napkin, then set it down. "Well, this is a special place you're going to go tonight. I can see some concern in your eyes, Bert, so I want you to know how special and safe the Presence Chamber is. It's just a way for us to come together as a town. To strengthen our bonds."

"But . . ." Bert sputtered. "But what happens? What do they do to us?"

Audrey laughed gently. "They don't do anything to you, Bert."

"Have you been there?" Jeffrey asked.

"Not yet. Remember, I've only been back here a couple months, and the Presence Chamber wasn't here when I was a child. But I want to go the very minute I'm able to. It's just that in Elderton the children come first. I'll have my chance to go once all you boys and girls have taken your turn for the year."

"Why can't you tell us more?" Bert asked, blanching. "Why's this such a big secret?"

Panic was beginning to layer itself over Bert's fear.

"It's just the way things are done. I know that sounds mysterious and all." She said the word "mysterious" in a playful manner, as if she were reading a bedtime story. "But that's just so everyone can have the experience on their own and keep it within them for their very own. Forever."

"Okay," Bert said. He'd closed down. He wasn't going to ask anything else. Knowing everything Bert had been through in the past, Audrey empathized with the boy's fear. After all, he'd been beaten by his father so many times that several angry monuments of scar tissue were still evident whenever he took off his clothes to bathe. No wonder he didn't trust adults.

She sighed, looking forward to later that night when the boys returned. Then, everything would be all right.

Jeffrey was changing into a nice new Chicago Cubs sweatshirt he'd found waiting on his bed when he noticed Bert stuffing items into a paper sack.

"What are you doing?"

Bert didn't even turn around. "I'm outta here, man. I'm leaving."

"Why?" Jeffrey was sincerely puzzled. He'd seen his share of untrustable characters during his years in foster care, even before. Miss Gayle wasn't one of them.

Bert interrupted his hasty packing and turned around to face Jeffrey. Jeffrey had never seen such uncertainty, such quiet dread, in another human's eyes.

" 'Cause something bad's gonna happen," Bert said. "I can feel it. Don't forget, kid, if I've learned one thing over the years, it's how to know when danger's on its way. Believe me, it's on its way. I don't know what it is and I don't know how it'll hurt us, but there's danger sneakin' up on us.

"Did you hear her talking in there?" Bert continued. "I mean, it sounds like this is a cult or something. Far as I know, we'd get out there and have to help them sacrifice a baby or eat a cat or something."

"Come on, Bert. You can't believe that."

Bert thrust one last shirt into the paper sack. "Don't you ever watch talk shows on TV? Little towns like this, they have their little cults. You get in, then you can't get out and you either end up dead or, if you're lucky enough to escape, you become a Fundamentalist. I don't know about you, but I don't want either of those things to happen to me. Better that I get a weekly beating and live with people I can predict."

"I don't understand you, Bert."

Bert rolled the paper sack until it was closed up tight, then tucked it under his arm. He strode quickly to the window and flung it open.

After he stuck his first leg outside, he stopped and looked Jeffrey in the eyes. "You oughta come with me, Jeffrey. Really."

"I'm staying here. Dangerous or not, I haven't felt this good in a long time."

Shaking his head, Bert said, "Do me one favor then, would you?"

"Anything."

Bert snaked the rest of the way outside, then stuck his head back in through the open window. "If something happens to me and I end up dead—"

"That's not going to happen."

"Still . . . if it does, I want you to make me a promise."

"What's that?"

"Tell me I'm dead. Just walk right up to me and say, 'Bert, you're a dead man.' I don't want to end up like Vida Proust. If I'm done, I'm done. Promise me."

"Sure, I guess. I promise. But, Bert—"

Bert melted into the gathering dusk.

Chapter Twelve

I wonder if I could plead temporary insanity if the whole town saw me hammering a blind man to death right on the town square. Sure. I could say that I thought he was going to kill me, or that his breath was toxic and caused hallucinations. Something—

"Where are we now?" the blind man asked.

Somehow the man had found his voice within the past fifteen minutes. Before that, all Ben got were the croaking whisper-sounds. Say, maybe this was the guy's job around town: spooking visitors, making sure that they would leave town in a cartoon blur and never return, keeping Elderton safe and unspoiled for future generations.

"We're on the west side of the square," Ben answered wearily. "How much longer do I have to lead you around? It's getting late. The sun's almost down. I'm sick of this."

The blind man ignored him. "Are we near the Rexall drug store? I like that place. I used to buy comic books there when I was little. Twelve cents, they cost."

"Yeah, that's just great."

Long ago, whatever fear and apprehension the blind man had elicited in Ben had dissolved. Now Ben just found him aggravating as hell, poorly mannered, poorly groomed, and holding on to Ben's arm just a wee bit too firmly.

Ben had hoped that upon driving the blind man into town, he could just let him off somewhere: the bowling alley, the grocery store, the county jail, somewhere the blind man would feel at home. No such luck. The walk they were taking was interminable it seemed, with no apparent goal other than to make Ben's existence a bleak, malodorous purgatory.

Twice, Ben had tried to escape, but each time the blind man aped every move Ben made and again clamped his hand around Ben's bicep. Resigned, Ben decided the best thing to do was to serve his sentence and pray for an early parole.

"Can you at least tell me who you are so I know what name to put on the lawsuit?"

"I'm nobody," the blind man said, facing straight ahead.

"Don't you recognize me?"

Well, at least the guy responded. That's something. Even if he is a non-sequitur-spewing smartass.

"Really," Ben said, "how about if I take you to the coffee shop? You'll know someone there. You can sit and relax, take the proverbial load off your stinky feet. I've got things to do, you know what I mean, Mr. Nobody?"

"Lead me," the blind man said.

They'd passed a few people as they circled the town square. While each would smile and nod, no one seemed the least bit impressed with the fact that this virtual stranger was leading a dirty, blind citizen around town. Ben hadn't even considered asking for help. Somehow he knew any request would be met with a bewildered stare or an intimation that he wasn't quite as compassionate as the rest of Elderton's denizens. The last thing he wanted to do was to alienate the townspeople, especially when there was an alien spacecraft waiting for him just outside of town. Better to bear the cross and not whine about the resulting backache any more than necessary.

"Okay," Ben said, "we're going to step off a curb here, then cross the street."

"Madison Street."

"Yeah, whatever."

They were halfway across the street when a car arrived at the intersection, bright headlamps trained on the two of them. Ben turned and shielded his eyes.

For a moment, the car sat there rumbling. Then Ben made out the make and model of the car and tasted a *soupçon* of relief.

"Harold!" Almo Parrish shouted as he got out of the passenger side of Chandler Quinn's fungus-colored Rambler. "Harold Brainard! Darn you!"

"That's it," the blind man said, brandishing his gap-filled smile. "*That's* my name: Harold Brainard."

"Wonderful . . . Harold," Ben said, scowling. "That's just the kitty-cat's damned meow."

Leaving the car running, headlamps glowing, Chandler also exited the car.

Ben's sense of relief heightened when Chandler and Almo walked up to him, looking perturbed at Harold Brainard. Rescued at last.

God, they should feel the Gordian knot in my *intestines right now if they want to know perturbed.*

Almo crossed his arms over his chest. "Let loose of him, Harold. Now!"

Harold Brainard did just that.

Unconsciously, Ben reached up and massaged his bicep, perhaps hoping to remove the tension. Or the smell.

Without uttering another word, Harold Brainard trooped the rest of the way across Madison Street, stepped confidently onto the curb, and within seconds had left the square, swallowed by shadows.

"I don't know how to thank you," Ben said.

Almo still looked dismayed. "Think nothing of it, Ben. How long have you been putting up with Harold?"

"Damn, I don't even know for sure. Seems like days."

Chandler let out a hearty laugh. "That Brainard chap certainly can be a plague."

"From what I've seen, I'd tend to agree with you," Ben said, smiling at the two men. Inside he was wondering whether they had found the alien who escaped the crash of its small craft. He also wondered how quickly he could ditch Almo and Chandler so he could make his way back to the creek where the ship lay and gather the evidence he needed. If things progressed apace, he'd be able to file a story within a day. Within two days, he'd be on every major news program and talk show. Within three days, he'd be *somebody*.

"Harold really doesn't personify potential discomfiture, you understand," Chandler said, a bemused smile angling his handlebar mustache.

"He's harmless," Almo translated.

"What's his story?" Ben asked.

"Back when he was a teenager," Almo said, "Harold was a champion gymnast, one of the best in the state."

"So true," rejoined Chandler. "The boy could spin and fly through the air like a preternatural ballerina . . . excuse me, ballerin*o*."

Almo nodded, then continued, "He was at the sectional tournament here in town. From what I've heard, he was dominating every event he participated in. Right before the final event of the evening, Harold stepped outside for a few moments to meditate, collect himself. There, he apparently saw something that chilled him to the bone."

"What was it?" Ben asked. He sensed another *Eye* story taking form.

"He's never said," Almo said. "That's the problem! If only he'd talked to us, any of us, I'm sure everything would have worked out fine. But he didn't. He wouldn't. And he still won't. He claims that his job is to forget . . . that is, when he remembers what his job is. Half the time he can't even remember his name."

"He was a blind gymnast, eh?" Ben asked, taking mental notes.

Chandler shook his head. "No, sir. As the last event commenced that night, he materialized in the fieldhouse . . . and he was blind."

"Someone blinded him while he was outside?"

Chandler shook his head.

"He blinded himself?"

Chandler nodded.

"How?" Ben asked, increasingly intrigued. "Acid or something?"

"As far as we can conjecture," Chandler said, "it was undiluted volition that blinded him."

Ben had trouble processing that, but it didn't surprise him. There were a lot of things in Elderton he couldn't process. "I don't get it."

"Neither do we," Almo said. "But it seems young Harold Brainard willed himself into blindness."

"Willed himself? Like . . . how? Hysterical blindness, is that what they call it? It's all psychological or something?"

"That's not it, my boy," Chandler said. "Doctor Trotter examined him. He's really blind. It's not merely an internal conflict without external manifestation. His eyes are verifiably nonfunctional."

Ben had never heard of such a thing. How was that possible? But there were other questions to ask if he were going to write the Harold Brainard story. "Why did he insist on my leading him around? It's obvious he knows this town like the back of his hand."

Almo shrugged. "I can't answer that either. Perhaps he

needs to go somewhere that he's never been. Perhaps he wants to see something he needs to see. He seems to be *looking,* as crazy as that sounds."

Chandler nodded his agreement. "And as far as why he selected you as his guide, he only demands this of visitors. Never citizens of Elderton."

"Long ago Chandler and I told him that we wouldn't lead him, and the rest of the community followed suit. He just needs to talk, to tell us what he saw that night. But he refuses."

"I see." Ben felt an internal head-shake. This stuff was fascinating but almost overwhelming in its implications. Not that Ben could pick out what the damned implications were.

Chandler walked closer and placed his hand on Ben's shoulder. "But the real reason we were foraging for you had nothing to do with the daunting Harold Brainard. What we'd like is for you to accompany us."

Possibility glistened in Ben's mind, immediately pushing aside any curiosity about the history or fate of Harold Brainard. At last he'd earned the trust of two men in town who likely held many secrets. He knew of one important secret they possessed. They'd seen the UFO, possibly even made contact with its occupant.

He didn't want to seem too anxious. "Well," Ben said, "why do you want me to come with you?"

Almo stepped near. "This town's in terrible danger. We need your help. Come with us. Let us tell you about it."

I need your help, too, but it's not about rescuing this screwy town. It's about saving my professional rectal cushion. I need to get back out to the pasture and wrest off a hunk of that spacecraft.

"Okay, I'll come with you," Ben said.

96

Both men looked relieved.

"But you have to remember, I'm a reporter. I want a story."

"You may be a reporter," Almo said, "but you're a hometown boy first."

Right.

Chapter Thirteen

"Are you sure you want to do this?" Standing in his kitchen, Chandler poured three snifters of brandy. He'd collared Almo and brought him in with him not because he needed assistance, but to allay his increasing concern.

"I don't see any choice," Almo said. "We're in danger, don't you understand?"

"Of course I do, my friend. I accredit your sapience. I know that Elderton's going to be invaded, perhaps already has been. But contemplate this for a moment: Ben Savitch freshly arrived in town. He's been poking around, trying to uncover secrets. It's obvious! And he's a reporter, for God's sake! Consider, I ask you: What if *he's* the invader?"

Almo shook his head, frowning. "I just don't see any choice. We have to have faith that Elderton's put more into him than the years he's spent away from us."

"Still—"

"You guys need any help in here?" Ben's head was sticking through the kitchen doorway. The smile he wore was much too ingratiating.

Chandler nearly spilled one of the drinks. "No, no, son. You go have a seat on the davenport. We'll be in presently."

Ben's head disappeared.

An imploring expression on his already-concerned face, Chandler said, "You're sure about this?"

"No, not sure. Just resigned."

The story of a lifetime was at hand, inches from his twitching journalistic fingertips. Ben felt it every bit as clearly as he smelled Harold Brainard's lingering odor.

He envisioned the two men walking in any moment, disclosing the fact that they'd found both the spacecraft and its occupant, and then revealing every last cosmic detail: where the alien was from, what malevolent designs he had on planet Earth, what he ate, what music he listened to. Everything. He hadn't felt this excited since the honeymoon with his second wife, Darla, the comely contortionist. At last—after nearly two decades of slogging along, barely eking out a living at innumerable newspapers—the pot at the end of the rainbow was visible.

He couldn't sit still. He stood up and walked to the front window of Chandler's living room, temporarily indifferent to the fact that it seemed every time he'd peered through a large window lately, something had been shambling past or staring back at him.

An engine backfired. An old cobalt-blue Ford truck chugged past.

Ben was not a man given to sudden visceral reactions. He had been through enough in his personal life alone to know how to step back and let a situation seep its way into him for proper analytic evaluation. Nonetheless, his stomach lurched.

Sitting in the back end of the truck were several children, each motionless save for the swaying that accompanied the truck's movements. Across each of their faces was tied a black blindfold.

Ben's mind shot back to a undercover series that his friend Wayne Sallee had written for *Chicago Rampant*, detailing how one South Side neighborhood had made a betting sport out of pitting deformed children against one another in fights to the death. Could that be what this was? Systematic child torture? Were Elderton's secrets darker than just a collection of harmless eccentricities? Was there more to hide than a crashed UFO?

Ben wasn't sure, but he was sure of something else. One of those children in the back of the truck was Jeffrey Sprague. There was no mistaking the boy's shock of bright red hair.

Jeffrey knew about the crashed UFO, or so he claimed. Perhaps they're eliminating all witnesses.

Perhaps I'm next.

There was no end to the secrets here, it seemed. Either that or Elderton, Illinois, was a geographical Rorschach inkblot, a display of maddening ambiguity upon which even a stony-hearted reporter could project both his deepest fears and boldest dreams.

"Here you go."

Ben was startled by Chandler's spirited voice, turned quickly away from the window, and accepted the snifter of brandy. Despite himself, he took a big gulp and forced down a mouthful of liquid flame.

"Before we go any further," Almo said, "Chandler would like to introduce you to someone he's brought into town to help us."

"Oh?" Ben said as nonchalantly as possible, although his voice cracked like a pre-pubescent choirboy's.

"That's right," said Chandler. "Ben Savitch, I'd like you to meet . . . Frank Shepard. Frank, come in here, would you please?"

The kitchen door swung open and a man walked in.

His blonde hair was neatly parted, shiny with Brylcreem. He was clad in a neatly tailored—though slightly out of date—double-breasted suit, crisply pressed with box-square shoulders. He even wore the trademark wire-rimmed glasses.

Ben's mouth hung open so widely that a softball could have been easily inserted. During the early to mid-sixties, Ben could be found every Saturday night at seven o'clock, sitting rock-still in front of the television as he watched the series featuring his favorite comic book superhero. Hell, once he had even made his very own cape from a beach towel and come this close to breaking his neck when he leapt from the garage roof, his goal being to enjoy a quick flying trip around the moons of Jupiter.

Chandler smiled. "You may remember him better as the star of television's . . ." Now Chandler cupped his hands around his mouth and shouted with the festive passion of an old-time announcer: *"Sky-Lord—Master of the Elements!"*

Good God.

It *was* Frank Shepard.

Chapter Fourteen

Jeffrey had become almost hypnotized on the way out of town. The truck's swaying, the wind whistling past his face, the high-pitched thrum of the engine: all of them conspired to transport him to a secret inner place.

He abruptly emerged from his trance when the truck took a sharp left turn. He lost his balance momentarily, falling into two or three children riding beside him.

"Ouch! Hey, watch it!"

"Jeez, you poked me in the eye!"

Feeling the familiar feelings of self-consciousness and embarrassment at his awkwardness, Jeffrey muttered a few apologies, then lay down in the truck's bed so he wouldn't be bobbing around anymore.

The truck jumped and careened, and no longer was there the sound of concrete or gravel beneath its tires. Weeds whispered against the truck's undercarriage. Paved roads had been left behind.

The truck slowed. Jeffrey took a deep breath and sat up.

He was ready. In fact, he couldn't remember the last time he had felt this sheer sense of expectancy. Maybe never. He was so glad the dog and he had found their way to Elderton, so happy that Vida Proust had taken him to school with her, so happy that the beautiful Miss Gayle had given him a place to live, so happy that he'd been invited to share in the Presence Chamber.

Life was good.

The truck shuddered to a stop. The engine backfired one final time, then died.

Being blindfolded, Jeffrey had noticed that in the short time it took them to arrive at their destination, his hearing had sharpened. As he took in a deep breath and held it, he could clearly hear the other children in the back of the truck doing the same.

"Children, we're almost ready for you," came the voice of the man who'd driven them.

Jeffrey heard the back gate of the truck being unlatched and lowered, then felt the shock absorbers giving as someone stepped up into the truck bed.

"Time to take off those blindfolds, young friends," said the man.

Jeffrey felt a smile spreading across his face. God, this was wonderful. This was life.

Large fingers grasped the satin ties at the back of Jeffrey's head. The bow was deftly untied, the blindfold lifted away. He blinked his eyes several times, then rubbed them.

"Hey, we made it," the boy sitting next to Jeffrey said, giving him a playful punch to the arm.

"Yeah," Jeffrey said. He stood up and surveyed the surroundings.

As best as he could tell, they were several miles outside of Elderton in a totally unpopulated area. They were surrounded on all sides by thick forestland, great masses of gigantic trees standing as silent sentries.

With one exception. There was a small building fashioned of crumbling brick, looking like it was built a long time ago. Its roof was partially collapsed, and many of its black shingles were torn and flapping in the wind. Through its windows bright light shone, and a warm yellow lamp illuminated the entryway.

"Okay, kids," the kind driver said. "Hop on out of the truck and follow me."

Jeffrey clambered out, his feet grateful to meet solid ground. Within him, anticipation swelled.

Miss Gayle said that this was a special place, that coming here would help him become a part of Elderton. That's what he wanted, more than anything. To become a part of a place that had let him belong, that had invited him to assume a new life role: the good kid, the one people liked, the one who belonged. The one who mattered.

Together, the children followed the man to the front door of the small building. When he reached the entryway, the man turned around, raised one hand, and asked for silence.

"Welcome," he said in a strong, resonant voice. "My name is Arthur Everett and this, boys and girls . . ." He swung one arm around with a dramatic flourish and pointed toward the front door. ". . . is the Presence Chamber, a special station that's been maintained and quietly celebrated for fifteen years. Most times, it seems like it's been here so long that no one could possibly remember how it all started."

A few whispered *wows* from the group.

Arthur Everett cleared his throat. Silence was restored.

"Now, children, what we're going to share with you tonight is the essence, the fabric of Elderton itself. You are a part of this community, each of you. And tonight, you'll become even more a part. It is my hope, and the hope of everyone in Elderton, that you'll appreciate and embrace what you're going to experience tonight."

Suddenly a horn honked behind them. The children turned.

Jeffrey's smile widened. It was Miss Gayle. How wonderful it would be to share this special night with her.

He heard her sweet voice. "Wait just a minute, please."

Then she crossed the headlight beams and grasped the hand of a little boy who had come out of the passenger side of her car. "Do you have room for one more?" she asked, and Jeffrey could feel the warmth in her voice. He hoped one day he'd marry someone as perfect as Miss Gayle.

"Well, sure," Arthur Everett said. "Always room for one more."

Jeffrey's jaw dropped when he saw who was with Miss Gayle.

Bert Frehley.

"Good evening, Jeffrey," Miss Gayle said. "Did you have a nice ride out here?"

"It was fun," he answered.

"Do you mind walking inside with your roommate, being his partner tonight?"

"No. That's fine."

Miss Gayle brought Bert to Jeffrey's side, patted them both on their shoulders, returned to her car, and drove away.

"Okay, children," Arthur Everett said, "let me answer any questions before we go inside."

Jeffrey turned toward Bert. "I thought you ran away," he whispered. "What happened?"

In the darkness he couldn't get a good look at Bert's face, but the boy's voice told him something was terribly wrong.

"Jeffrey," Bert said, voice coarse and flat. "Help me, Jeffrey."

Jeffrey leaned closer to Bert. No longer did Bert look frightened or determined. He looked . . . well, he barely looked like he was there at all.

"Help me, Jeffrey," Bert repeated.

"Why? What's the matter with you?"

"Look."

105

Bert slowly unzipped his coat, then unbuttoned the top two buttons of his shirt.

"Look," he said again.

As a few of the children asked friendly questions of Arthur Everett, Jeffrey leaned closer and closer, until his nose was no more than two inches from Bert's chest.

He almost threw up. There was a horrible gash. No, it was worse than a gash, so dreadful looking that Jeffrey didn't know what to call it. It was as though someone had grabbed hold of Bert's skin and pulled him apart. Ragged edges traced the deep wound that ran at least ten inches down his chest.

"Tell me," Bert said.

"What happened to you?"

"Look," Bert said, "it's not bleeding."

"Yeah. What happened though?"

"Tell me, Jeffrey."

"Tell you what?"

"Tell me I'm dead."

"Wha—?"

"Okay," Arthur Everett called. "Is everyone ready to go inside?"

"Tell me, Jeffrey. Please tell me. Tell me I'm dead."

Jeffrey didn't need a medical degree to know that what Bert was saying was true. Not only was the ghastly wound on his chest not bleeding, but Bert's skin was slack, even on his face. Slack, and almost frozen. And there was a slight but unmistakable odor, one of those smells you don't have to be taught about, a smell that a deep part of every human knows.

"Tell me, Jeffrey. Please."

The crowd was starting to move, shuffling at a reverent pace.

"Jeffrey. Tell me."

106

So Bert had been right. There *was* danger in Elderton. And from the looks of it, not only had Bert been killed but, worse yet, after he was killed he wasn't even allowed to die. Even Jeffrey's nameless dog had been granted a better fate than that.

Hot tears spilled down Jeffrey's cheeks. For the first time in years, he had felt like he'd found a home, a sanctuary, a place where he could grow and prosper, become a human being who was thought of as kind and smart, become a grown-up whom his parents would be proud of were they alive. A place where he belonged.

During his years of foster care, he had tried to enter each new placement with hopefulness, a positive attitude. Always before he'd been bitterly disappointed. Now it seemed this place he'd chosen for himself wasn't any different. Maybe it was even worse, since its danger was dressed up in friendly smiles and tender words and pats on the back and talk of gentle, quiet magic.

"Tell me, Jeffrey."

He only had a second to decide and, at times like that—when options swirl through the mind like mad bees—instinct rushes to the fore.

So Jeffrey did two things.

He whispered, "You're dead" to Bert and watched with terror as Bert began to visibly stiffen, to lose his balance.

At first, none of the other children seemed to notice, so intent they were on entering the Presence Chamber. Then one girl happened to glance in Bert's direction. She stopped in her tracks, slapped a hand over her mouth and pointed.

"Look!" she squealed.

As everyone turned to see what was wrong, Bert didn't so much fall as plunge to the ground, hitting the pavement like he, too, was made of concrete.

He was still, more still than being asleep or even unconscious, the kind of still that Jeffrey's mother had been on that nightmare afternoon in May.

The second thing Jeffrey did was run. He savored the adrenaline coursing through his body, giving him strength and speed and focus at the same time it pushed away the horror.

A forest lay just ahead. An easy place in which to get lost, or to lose others. He couldn't be captured now, not in a million years.

It felt like his life depended on it.

It felt like he was flying.

Chapter Fifteen

After his journey with Ben Savitch had been frustrated by the arrival of Almo Parrish and Chandler Quinn, Harold did something he hadn't done before, at least as far as he could remember, which wasn't all that far.

He kept walking, no longer tracing and retracing the familiar routes he had traveled for so many years. On his cheeks he felt the glow of the streetlights steadily dimming as he trod farther and farther from the courtyard square.

He knew each crack and crevice on every sidewalk in town as clearly as he knew the angles of his own body. As he continued walking, feeling himself blanketed by night's shadows, even the sidewalks became less and less familiar.

Soon there were no sidewalks at all.

He found himself at the edge of a vast forest. He felt the presence of the mass of towering trees before him—swaying and dancing and rustling in the gentle wind—extending into infinity.

He sat down on the moist, spongy ground, crossed his legs in front of him, and began to weep. He thought it was the first time he'd cried in twenty years, and he wasn't sure why it was happening.

"Harold Brainard, Harold Brainard," he muttered to himself between stifled sobs, hopeful that by repeating his name, he wouldn't forget it again. "Harold Brainard, Harold Brainard . . ."

With every molecule of his will he tried to keep hold of the words that Almo and Chandler had spoken when they'd interrupted his journey with Ben Savitch tonight, when they had presented Harold's history as easily and smoothly as if they were reciting it from memory, giving a lecture they'd presented a thousand times.

"Harold Brainard, Harold Brainard, Harold Brainard, Harold Brainard . . ."

He persisted in repeating his name, a mantra to his mutable identity, over and over and over again.

Suddenly, long-absent memory filled him like a swallowed sun.

He remembered that night, the night of the county gymnastics tournament back in '77, the one Almo and Chandler had described in vague, titillating terms.

He smiled, and his tears flowed over his lips, coating his tongue with bitter brine. That moment, he was transported to that distant time when his body was strong and lithe, his emotions stable and composed, his spirit hopeful and sanguine.

Alive.

He recalled the sweet feeling of victory, of certainty in himself and his gifts. He had been close to tears that night because, for the first time, he'd realized how much of what he possessed as a human being was a gift from Elderton: its quiet, gentle, nonpossessive magic that could as easily be ignored as embraced. The way everything moved along like it was written by a hand larger than any ever imagined, a story of cooperation and touch, smiles and encouragement. A story of hope.

He had become so excited that he'd had to step outside of the fieldhouse, just to gather himself together, to prevent himself from becoming overwhelmed by the gratitude, the sea of emotions swelling and roiling inside him. He'd taken several deep breaths, trying to remember to focus. There was one more event that night, the biggest, most important event in his life.

As he had looked out upon the quiet roads of Elderton, filled with the feelings of grace and sanity that he'd never before fully realized were inside him . . . it happened.

As he experienced it now, the image was unclear, as if he were gazing at it through a dirty, cracked window.

Loud, crashing sounds.

An explosion.

A fireball, so large it looked like a blazing Earth rising up from the pavement. His eyes locked on the horrid sight.

And Elderton's magic, that instant, had disappeared for Harold Brainard.

Tears obscuring his vision, he'd raised his head, averting his gaze, hearing the screams and shouts and sirens.

"Nooooooooo!" he'd shrieked at the top of his lungs. "Nooooooooo!"

He'd stumbled around shouting for a few moments.

He couldn't see.

Just like that, he couldn't see anymore, as if his spirit insisted on time and distance in order to make sense of the drama that had just played out before him.

Darkness. Black. Nothing.

A heavy curtain drawn across life.

Just like that.

Blind.

Now, sitting in the forest, he shook his head, wiped his hands across his long-sightless eyes.

"My God," Harold Brainard said. "My God."

It had been easier, he realized, to forget all he had seen, to forget his name, to become the local annoyance, the one who disturbed anyone who managed to intersect his path. Yes. Easier than remembering what he'd seen.

Perhaps he'd find an answer here, outside the city limits,

in the dense, perfumed timberland. There had to be an answer somewhere.

He sniffed twice, got to his feet, and resumed walking.

He should have known by now that the answer wasn't going to be found in Elderton. He'd been searching there for so long.

"Harold Brainard, Harold Brainard, Harold Brainard . . ." he said, stepping deftly between trees and through gathering heaps of dead leaves.

Remembering.

"Harold Brainard, Harold Brainard . . ."

Chapter Sixteen

Crouched high in the tree, tiny feet balanced on opposing limbs, arms wrapped around the oak's mighty body, the entity lingered as it had so many times before, on so many worlds.

Waiting for the moment.

Contact. Connection. Meaning.

Memory burst inside it briefly, then flamed out.

Yes. This always happened. The moment. The contact. The union.

The meaning.

Squinting, it regarded the glorious harvest moon hovering overhead. Such simple, noble radiance. How fortunate everyone here was to be able simply to turn their heads upward and drink in such luscious beauty whenever they wanted.

Footsteps.

Yes.

The entity hugged the tree more tightly now, resting its cheek against the rough, wet, welcoming bark.

And waited.

The cool breeze played across its skin, caressing it, kissing it.

Not just one set of footsteps.

Two. From different directions.

Soon, something would happen, the entity realized.

Something that mattered.

Waiting.

Part Two

Tabloid Rapture

Chapter Seventeen

Ben drove to the Elderton Public Library, a small but princely brick building on the south side of the square, nestled between Jeanne's Alteration Shop and Mookie's Laundromat (which were equally small, stately and made of brick).

Other than a librarian keeping herself busy nose-down behind the shiny oaken counter, the place was empty save for two rooms full of bulging bookcases.

Ben took possession of a hard chair behind a corner table that was so shiny with wax he could count the number of spidery vessels in the reflection of his bloodshot eyes.

He pulled a stack of copies of *The Elderton Pilot* from the bookcase next to the table, and started flipping through them. That moment, perhaps more than any moment in memory, he needed to feel the soft, welcome scrape of paper and newsprint against his fingers. A reality anchor.

Too many days like this one and I'll be spending an involuntary six months in the Ha-Ha Hotel, the Manic Monastery, the Psychotic Pslammer.

It was bad enough that Almo and Chandler had spoken to him in hushed, conspiratorial tones, imploring him to stand with them and the town as it was invaded by some malevolent unknown force, the nature of which they hadn't an inkling.

It was bad enough that they had bedeviled his journalistic curiosity by admitting that they'd found the spacecraft, and hinting—though never admitting—that they knew where the alien might be located.

All of that would have been quite enough, thank you very much.

But then these two beanbags had to parade out a Frank Shepard look-alike. The guy looked so perfect it had Ben going for a minute. But as with everything else within this carnival of dim souls, it was an illusion, some guy who probably worked at the old JCPenney's on the east side of the square—Men's Goods—and just happened to possess the handsome jawline and chiseled facial features of television's Sky-Lord.

What did these people take Ben for? A total pinhead?

Paging through a recent issue of the *Elderton Pilot* he enjoyed, at least for a few fugitive moments, a sense of journalistic superiority. After all, the biggest local stories during the past month involved an old tree falling on an alderman's stately old brick house, the installation of the first traffic light in the county (smack dab in front of the Dog N' Suds), and the reunion of the Spandly clan who claimed to have perfected a mutant strain of savory eggplant, which they would protect until every last member of the proud family had died and gone to that big compost heap in the sky, by gum.

But as he continued turning the pages, Ben felt his brow wrinkling into a frown. He had the inescapable feeling that something was missing.

And suddenly, he knew what it was—well, why wouldn't he? After all, he'd spent dreadful months scripting obituaries for the *Peoria Journal-Star*, forever searching for some way to be proud of the craftsmanship necessary to bring lively prose to the lifeless.

He whipped past more pages, picked up more issues, flipped through those, too.

I'll be dipped.

118

There wasn't one obituary. Not one. Nada. Zippo. *Nothing.*

The sympathetic-looking librarian—candy-red hair pulled into a tight bun—wandered over to Ben's table, perhaps perplexed at the energy with which he was tearing through the local weekly.

She adjusted her cat-eye-rimmed glasses. "Can I help you, sir?" she asked, voice satiny and quiet, befitting her profession. "Anything in particular you're looking for?"

"Uh, no." What would be the use of letting her know that he wasn't finding any death notices in the local paper? Hell, an educated librarian probably picked up things like that.

More and more, it seemed to Ben that he had wandered into the heart of an elaborate joke, and only he was being kept ignorant of the punchline or, hell, even the setup for that matter.

Better to not let on how bizarre he was finding all this. He didn't need any more complications right now.

She smiled and winked. "Well, if you decide you need anything, just let me know. I'm not busy at all." She swept her hand around, italicizing the lack of patrons. "It's a good thing I'm a seamstress. I spend most of my days here just sewing up a little storm."

"Nice."

"I'm Mary Harmon," she said, presenting a limp hand, palm down.

Ben clasped it. "Ben Savitch. Pleased to meet you."

"Say, do you need any clothes? A nice shirt? Vest? Slacks? I can even cuff them, you know. I can sew anything."

"Thanks anyway," Ben said. "If I stay around town long enough, maybe I'll come back and have you do an entire suit for me. Hell, double-breasted, even."

119

She blushed, then started off.

Suddenly Ben was pinched by inspiration. "Oh, Miss . . . Mary?"

She turned around, smiled and winked again. "Yes?"

"Do you carry the *Peoria Journal-Star*, by any chance?"

Her face displayed the tiniest frown.

"I used to work there," he added quickly. "I'd like to see how the paper's doing without me."

The frown inverted itself. "Oh, I see. Well, I think there may be a stack back here somewhere."

Ben followed her into an adjoining room, where ceiling-high metal shelves held pristine, seemingly unread copies of *Time, Newsweek, Sports Illustrated, Life, People,* even *Rolling Stone*.

Not a single copy of *The Astonished Eye*, though.

The librarian had to get down on her hands and knees to locate the mountain of *Journal-Stars* jammed into the bottom corner of one shelf.

She grunted as she slid one pile out onto the floor.

Ben picked them up. "Thanks for your trouble, Mary."

"I'm happy you want to take a look at these. I don't remember the last time someone asked to see a paper other than the *Pilot*. Makes me feel like I'm doing my job."

"And doing it well, I might add."

She blushed again. "Why, thank you, Ben. I have years and years of the *Journal-Star* in the back room if you want to see them, too." A little eyelash flutter.

It's too bad I'm not in the market for a love mate. Let that bun down, throw away the cat-eye glasses, and this one might just be a wild jungle temptress. Hell, she could sew up her own leopard-skin dress and everything. Although she'd never be a Darla . . .

Ben carried the stack of newspapers to his table, set them

down, set himself down, then pulled the first issue off the top.

God, she was right. These papers were in mint condition. No one had so much as opened them. Not one dog-eared page. Not even a mouse-eared page.

Nothing.

He spent the next several minutes leafing through recent issues. It made him feel more grounded to scan articles about horrid house fires, malignant political scandals, factory explosions, ten-car pile-ups, abusive parents, and pernicious puppy mill owners.

Ahhhhh. All is *still right with the world.*

By the time he had burrowed down through three weeks' worth of the daily newspaper, he was sporting a big, knowing grin on his face, grateful that the little town of Elderton—and the strangeness he had stumbled into here—had not defiled the outside world.

His smile was swelling into a laugh when he turned a page and an article grabbed him by the mental lapels and jerked him close.

ELDERTON GIRL DIES AFTER FALLING INTO WELL

Elderton, Illinois—The body of eleven-year-old Vida Proust, the daughter of Phil and Elizabeth Proust of Elderton, was discovered early this morning at the bottom of an abandoned well, after community members and personnel of the Tri-County Rescue Team spent three days searching the countryside for her. She had last been seen when she attended a birthday party last Saturday night.

"We're not sure what happened yet," a shaken Rescue Team Coordinator Patrick Steinman said. "Apparently she was playing out here and just fell in. It's hard to picture how this could have happened."

Ben felt the blood draining out of his face and pooling in the pit of his stomach where it sat, burbling.

There she is. Sure as shit.

To one side of the article was a photograph of the little girl, the same little girl Ben had seen stumbling past Duane and Joyce's Coffee Shop, the little girl about whom Almo Parrish commented, "Vida hasn't been feeling well for a couple of weeks. Don't worry about her. We're keeping an eye on her. We'll take care of her. We take care of our own around here."

You sure as hell do.

Chapter Eighteen

"You mustn't lose hope, dear. Please." Almo sat next to Audrey at her kitchen table, his eyes filled with concern, a hand resting on her back. "There there, honey."

She couldn't stop crying. Her head lay on her crossed arms in front of her; her shoulders shook. Almo had found her this way when he arrived ten minutes earlier.

He sat back in his chair, sighed deeply and steepled his fingers in front of him.

Slowly, Audrey raised her head and focused her blood-shot, streaming eyes on the last Munchkin. When she finally spoke, her voice was informed with an edge of anger Almo had never before heard from her.

"Hope, Almo?" she said, shaking her head. "Hope? In what?"

"Hope in what we have here in Elderton."

"Have you ever heard of *false* hope?"

The words stung him, and he flinched. "Sure, Audrey, I've heard the term. But if there's one thing I've learned, it's this: there is no such thing as false hope. You hear me? *No such thing as false hope.* Hope is not a fact, not a principle, not a theorem, not a mathematical formula. The notion of truth or falseness doesn't apply. Hope, my dear, is a decision."

"Think of what's happened. It makes it pretty hard to hope."

"I know right now it doesn't look good—"

Audrey's eyes flared. "Doesn't look good? Yes, I'd say it doesn't look good. One of my boys has run away, and one of them is . . . is . . ."

123

"I know, I know." He stroked the back of her neck. "But that wasn't your fault and it wasn't Elderton's fault. The boy fell through a window trying to sneak out of the school after breaking into it."

"But ask yourself why it happened! Almo, he was at the school to pick up the few belongings he had in this world. He was running away because Elderton frightened him. He thought something horrible was going to happen at the Presence Chamber. When the janitor walked into the room, poor Bert must have panicked. He was scared, Almo, so scared. This magic you're always talking about, what good has it done Bert Frehley? Tell me that. Tell me how the magic is doing any of us any good."

"All I can say is I'm doing my best, honey. Chandler and I have been working hard to try and prepare ourselves, prepare the town—"

"For this invasion you talk about again and again?" The tears had stopped. She raised an index finger to keep time with her words. "Almo, I left this town to go to college, then taught in so many towns and cities before I returned to try and give a little something back to my hometown, to try and build a nest for myself. When I left, Elderton was quiet, peaceful, close-knit. People cared for one another, kept each other going. It made for a wonderful life. The magic I remember here was *that* magic, not . . . this other stuff. When I was growing up here, there wasn't any prediction of the first falling leaf, there wasn't any Presence Chamber, no impending invasions. Today, *you're* the center of the magic in this town. You're the one it comes through. To me, it looks more and more like *you're* the invader. *You're* the one who threatens Elderton, whether you mean to or not."

Face gone ashen, Almo got up and waddled to the door. "I understand your grief, Audrey. I understand how everything looks like a big mess to you right now. It *is* a big mess. But things are looking up. Tonight, Chandler and I enlisted the assistance of Ben Savitch. Perhaps he can help us. Perhaps he has gifts the rest of us lack."

"Who?" The anger melted from Audrey's face and was replaced with an expression of curiosity. "Did you say Ben Savitch? Benny Savitch?"

"Why, yes. He lived here as a young child. Neither Chandler nor I can remember him at all. But you do?"

"Yes," she said. "We were in the same first grade class, but—"

"Well, for heaven's sake. That's wonderful."

"He's back? I don't believe it. I never thought he'd come back. His family moved to northern Illinois. I remember how that surprised everyone, them leaving like that. I sure never expected to see him again. And you enlisted his help . . . to do what?"

"In return for helping us to stave off the invasion, whatever form that ends up taking, we've agreed to allow him to bring a camera and accompany Chandler and me on our hunt for the alien. We've already found the spacecraft, and Ben desperately wants the story."

Audrey's eyes were searching the ceiling. She was almost smiling. "Benny Savitch coming home. Maybe this place is magical after all."

Almo walked to Audrey and patted her on the back. "You'll be feeling better soon, sweetheart, I promise. Now I should tell you that Milo and Arthur buried the boy's body out behind the Presence Chamber. We couldn't think of anything better. Perhaps you can visit him, take some flowers and leave them there for him. Do what it takes to start healing."

"I think I will," Audrey said absently, almost as if she'd

completely forgotten the anger of only a few moments earlier. She barely seemed to know Almo was there anymore. "I think I'll do that. Thank you."

Face crinkled into a Munchkin grin, Almo let himself out of the house.

Something has to be done, Audrey thought. *Since I've come home, I've just been floating along, accepting everything strange that happens, being a part of my hometown in the only way I knew how, by accepting and smiling and going along. No more. The moment I heard about Vida Proust, then saw her with my own eyes, I should have taken action. The poor girl's been stumbling around town and I just pretended like nothing was happening. What could I have been thinking?*

She went to the closet, got her coat, and headed out to find Ben Savitch.

If he wanted the story of Elderton, he'd get it. She'd help him find it. After all, now she was looking for answers, too, having realized that even she was no longer sure what was going on.

And Audrey, she'd gain something: contact with someone who was living in the real world, who could sympathize with her and help her on the road back to the sanity she'd apparently left behind when she'd moved back to Elderton.

Compared to whatever it was that inhabited Elderton today, the magic she remembered was so much better— quieter, more full of love—and now she wasn't sure whether the magic existed at all anymore.

Chapter Nineteen

Ben lay on his back in the slab-like motel bed, head propped up on wafer-thin pillows wadded up into softball-sized spheres, a mound of *Peoria Journal-Star*s balanced across his thighs.

When he had asked the librarian if he could check out a random sampling of issues, she was more than happy to assist him. In fact, it was hard for him to resist taking the entire collection as she'd suggested. He wasn't sure if she were just a motivated librarian, or if his complimentary disposition had awakened, deep within her, something feral, Amazonian, and jungle-born. It was satisfying just to know the latter was a theoretical possibility.

He vised the telephone's handset between his shoulder and ear as he simultaneously dialed Max's number and looked through random issues of the *Journal-Star*, locating a few of his impeccably crafted obituaries in the process.

A sexy voice answered the phone.

"Yeah, give me Max Thomason. It's Ben Savitch calling."

Surprisingly, she put him through to Mr. Big Shot Television Superstation Anchorman without the normal grilling to which Ben had grown accustomed.

Too bad. This time he'd been ready.

Yeah, this is Ben Savitch. I'm a reporter for The Astonished Eye. *You may have heard of us. Well, I've located a crashed UFO and I was wondering if Mr. Thomason would be interested in some exclusive footage. Yeah, I'll hold . . . for exactly one minute and not a nanosecond more, babycakes.*

"Yeah, hi, Ben."

Maxipad's voice immediately chafed Ben's nerves. He could identify that tone: rushed, busy, too busy for an old friend to be distracting and annoying him.

"Max, I can tell you're busy, so I won't keep you long."

"Really?" A smartass chuckle.

"Yeah, stick it up your Q-meter, Walter Klondork. Seriously, Max, I've got something this time that'll give you a chubby if you're still capable of such physical reactions."

A sigh. An irritated and irritating sigh. "What is it, Ben?"

"Listen up, buddy. Not only have I found but I've *seen* the crashed UFO. I touched the goddamned thing! And I've made a deal with a couple of the local Gomers: they're going to give me exclusive coverage of this thing. So, how about it? Send down a camera crew, interview me—hell, *hire* me—and you'll have the biggest story of your career. You'll blow a hernia carrying all your awards."

"Yeah?"

It sounded like Maxipad was doing something else, flipping through a Rolodex while only pretending to listen.

Probably looking up INSANE ASYLUMS, INVOLUNTARY, DOWNSTATE.

"Max, sweeps week isn't all that far away. Do you have something better than this? C'mon, come clean, Padman."

"Ben, if this is along the lines of that Bigfoot—"

"Hell, no! As soon as I saw that photo, I identified it as a lumberjack in a ratty ape suit, didn't I?"

"No, not right away."

"Well, pretty damned quickly. But this is different. Aren't you listening? I touched the goddamned thing!"

It sounded like Max was stifling a yawn. "Tell you what, Ben. You get a piece of that spaceship and FedEx it to me, and I'll be happy to have an expert take a—"

Click.

"Bastard," Ben muttered, replacing the telephone on the bedstand.

He wiped the stack of newspapers off his legs, stood up and began pacing the room. "Okay, okay, I'll show the Pad a thing or two. I'll just go and get a hunk of the craft and give the story to one of the networks. Yeah, that's it. Maybe next time Maxipad Thomason will listen to his faithful old friend."

A sharp series of knocks on the door.

Ben nearly jumped, then collected himself so quickly it surprised him. After only a brief time in town, his nervous system had become more pliant.

He put his fists on his hips. "If it's you, Harold Brainard, I'm done leading you around this town! Got it?"

"It's not Harold Brainard," a singsong voice said from outside. "It's Audrey Gayle. We went to school together."

Although Ben had no idea who Audrey Gayle was, her voice was beautiful enough to encourage him to walk up to the cracked full-length mirror hanging askew on one wall and check his appearance. Unfortunately, the sole thing he noticed was the motif of smelly, finger-shaped grease marks on the sleeve of his shirt. "Thanks a lot, Harold," he muttered.

He opened the door and the first thought he had was that if this was the level of classmate he'd enjoyed while living in Elderton, he couldn't imagine why his early years were such a void. She was sumptuous, her beautiful face framed by short blond hair, her supple body clad in blue leggings and a sweater. Her smile shone.

"Hi," she said, somewhat shyly. "Do you remember me?"

God, she's gorgeous. Achingly so. I'm dyin' here. Darla? Who's Darla?

He had an impulse to lie but, being an astute journalist, knew the treacherous nature of follow-up questions. So he said, "You know, I'm sorry, I don't. You'll have to forgive me. I just got back into town and the memories of those days haven't flooded me yet. But gosh, I hope they do. Especially now."

She offered her hand and he shook it.

Audrey remained there expectantly, blue eyes wide, until Ben realized that he was standing in place like a Chicago stockyard clump. "Oh, sorry. Would you like to come in?"

While she stepped inside, Ben scampered to the only chair in the room and removed the heap of underwear, tossing them into a far corner.

Audrey sat down, too polite to acknowledge that she was placing her perfect body on a chair that only seconds ago had played host to soiled undergarments.

"I came for a couple of reasons," she said.

"Yes?" Ben said, adolescently excited even to his own ears.

"Once I heard you were in town, I just had to see you. We were in the same first grade class. Miss Harnaker's? I thought it would be nice to reminisce. I always wondered what happened to you."

"Sure." He had no clue, not a dollop of memory about Miss Harnaker or Audrey Gayle, but he didn't sense a follow-up question on the horizon, being astute and all.

"But there's something even more pressing."

An obscene response leapt into Ben's mind, but he nudged it aside.

"What's that, Audrey?" he asked.

"There's something very strange happening in Elderton. Everything is falling apart."

"God, am I glad to hear you say that," Ben said, appreciating the smooth sanity of Audrey's words. "You don't know how glad. I was beginning to think I was losing my mind."

"You're not."

Ben experienced a flurry of desires and tugs that moment. Making an instant decision to blend them, he asked, "Have you heard about the crashed UFO?"

"Yeah, I've heard a little."

"I'll tell you what: why don't you come with me. I'm going to drive out to the crash site. We can reminisce about the old days, discuss the weirdness in Elderton, and pick up a UFO, all in one trip. How many times in life will that combination of recreational activities present itself?"

"Not often, I'm sure," she said, face widening into an irresistible smile. "What do you want to do when we get there?"

Another fleeting obscene thought, harder to extinguish than the first.

Nope, can't do it. Focus. Hands on the reins, Ben. Grip that rudder. Eyes on the prize.

He leaned close and whispered, "I've already found the UFO. It's small, it's light. I want to bring it back . . . here."

Chapter Twenty

Sky-Lord seemed a mite depressed.

"Come on, Frank," Chandler said, clenching his pipe between his teeth. "You're never going to reclaim your superhero stature unless you strive like the god-man you are. Now, give it the old college try, my disconsolate friend."

Frank Shepard loosened his tie, took off his eyeglasses, then removed his square-shouldered suit coat and conscientiously laid it across the arm of a chair. "All right, Mr. Quinn, if you say so."

Frank leaned forward, narrowed his eyes, and stared intently at the bowl of Chandler's pipe for what seemed like several minutes.

Chandler's eyes remained every bit as riveted to the target as Frank's.

Then, like a kindling sprite, small diamond-shaped sparks leapt from Frank's eyes and into Chandler's pipe bowl. A corkscrew of smoke arose from the tobacco.

Chandler sat back in his chair, eyes as wide as cookies. "There, you see? You see? There it is! Your power of thunderbolt vision manifested itself! You see?"

Frank bunched up his eyebrows. "Uh, yes. I guess so." He didn't seem nearly as impressed as Chandler.

"What's the problem, my reanimated chum?"

Frank shook his head like he was trying to clear it. "I'm sorry, Mr. Quinn, but . . . where did you say we are?"

"Elderton, Illinois, Frank. Now listen closely. I reanimated you from a videotape of a television program in which you starred. Don't you remember me explaining all this?"

"Kind of. So I'm alive?"

"More or less. But don't become bedeviled about your existential status right now. Don't you see what potential you have? I mean, you effected the lighting of my pipe just by gazing at it. Your capacities are returning."

"I have powers." Frank Shepard spoke the words not as a question, but as a statement he was trying desperately to absorb and accept. "I have powers."

"Yes, Frank, powers. And you haven't seen anything yet. By the time Elderton is invaded, you will be a fully fortified flyboy, my friend. Once again, you shall be 'Master of the Elements!' "

"We're going to be invaded and I'm going to help." Same monotone, still trying to orient himself.

"That's utterly correct." Getting up from his chair, Chandler flung his hand toward the ceiling. "Here, get up, Frank. Up up up. Let's try something else. You need to venture a bit further into your galaxy of preternatural powers."

A bewildered expression contorting his face, Frank rose from the chair and stood at attention, as if in his haze of confusion he had relinquished the last relics of his free will.

Chandler placed his hands on his knees and hunkered down like a wrestling coach. "Now, Frank . . . fly!"

"Fly?"

"Yes, fly. Permit yourself to abscond the constraining shackles of gravity. C'mon, you can do it! Believe in me. Believe in yourself, dear Frank!"

Frank looked down at the floor, then toward his hands. He shook his head slightly, questioning.

A minute passed. Chandler's neck was straining with excitement, cable-taut. His clenched fist trembled.

"You can do it, boy!"

Slowly, slowly, Frank floated off the floor.

One inch. Two.

Still staring at the floor, his hands. Confused.

Three inches. Four.

"Yes!" Chandler cried. "Oh, yes, my floating associate!"

Like a feather above a candle's flame, Frank Shepard gracefully lifted into the air.

"Magnificent, Frank! You're doing marvelously!"

Almo walked into Chandler's front room, having let himself in the back door. Seeing the reanimated Frank Shepard defying gravity, he patted Chandler on the shoulder. "Well, I'll be."

Chandler laughed giddily. "It is something to behold, isn't it, my *petite confrere?*"

"So he's remembering his powers?"

Chandler shrugged. "It comes and goes, but I think by actively working with him, he'll be renewed by the time we're invaded."

"Wonderful. We've got no time to lose. I can feel the danger increasing every hour, every minute."

Chandler bent down and whispered, "I do have one concern though, my friend."

"What's that?"

"Look at Frank."

"I am. He's floating off the ground."

"No, look even closer. Zero in on his . . . edges."

"I don't underst—"

"Almo," Chandler said, "he's flickering around the edges."

Sure enough, the reanimated Frank Shepard's body was less clear, less substantial than it had been when he first appeared. The very perimeter of his body was shimmering ever so subtly, as if it were short-circuiting or fading out.

"His margins are leaking," Chandler added thoughtfully.

"What does that mean?" Almo asked.

Chandler put his hand on the last Munchkin's back, and guided him toward the kitchen.

"It means he's unstable, I guess. So in a way I'm happy the invasion is apparently occurring soon. At this point I can't say how long Frank—as we know him—will exist."

They had just reached the threshold of the kitchen when a loud crashing sound echoed through the house.

Together, Chandler and Almo turned and hurried back into the living room.

Where they found Frank Shepard crumpled face-down on the floor.

"My goodness, Frank, are you all right?" Chandler said, kneeling.

"I don't know what's happening to me," Frank said, face buried in his arms. Raising his head, he turned toward Chandler, eyes moist with tears. "I want to be what you want me to be, Mr. Quinn. I want to help you. I want to be a hero. But something's happening. Something doesn't feel right."

Chandler reached down and gently massaged Frank's shoulder blade. "I know, my friend. I know."

Now Frank's fringes were flittering and twinkling even more, looking like the ragged edges of unraveling fabric.

Chapter Twenty-One

Harold Brainard stopped walking and stood motionless in the forest.

A lone barn owl hooted in the distance, an aria of loneliness. Leaves whispered to one another in autumn conversation.

Since he had no vision to distract him, when he closed his eyes it was solely out of habit.

There. Again.

Footsteps in the grass, first sweeping through the dying blades, then halting.

Sweeping.

Halting.

"Hello?" Harold said.

Hearing no response, he raised his head and sniffed the air.

Yes, there was a faint scent here, floating delicately on dusk's lazy breeze.

It was not the smell of the trees or the grass, or of moisture on the wind. It wasn't the odor of dying vegetation, of leaves curling and turning on their boughs.

It was something else. Something alive.

"Hello?" Harold repeated.

He smiled as invitingly as possible and, as he did, pictured himself as that young boy in high school, face full of freshness and innocence and wide-eyed marvel. He hadn't seen himself since those days. He wondered what he looked like now.

Then a rush of electricity crackled through his body,

every nerve fiber sparking simultaneously, like a holy string of Christmas lights.

His body stiffened, his fists clenched.

Then, inside his head, he heard the voice. *What do I look like?*

The voice was gentle, melodious, even though it was strange. It sounded like someone singing three different notes at once, in perfect harmony.

Momentarily, Harold couldn't catch his breath. He squeezed his eyes even more tightly shut, wrapped his arms around himself and concentrated. Finally he was able to say, "I don't know what you look like. I'm blind."

What happens now?

"I don't know. I can't even see you. Here, come closer. Let me touch you."

Harold heard a skittering in the grass, like a toddler skipping.

I am here.

Trembling, Harold knelt and extended his hand, palm out. Upon making first contact, he instinctively pulled back. The skin—if that's what it was—was warm. But it felt like highly polished cherry wood, without a pit or irregularity, just a whorling pattern of grain. Not like skin at all.

He touched again. This time he left his hand there.

That is me, said the voice inside his head.

"Yes," Harold said, his tone reverent. "I feel you."

Tell me who I am.

"I don't know."

Tell me who you are.

"I'm . . . I'm . . . my name is . . ."

Whether it was his absorption in the moment or the recurring amnesia that had plagued him all these years, his name—and everything else about him—had once again flittered away like a startled sparrow.

"I don't know," Harold finally answered.

What do I do now?

"I don't know."

Harold stood, then reached out with his hand.

Small fingers closed around it.

"Let's walk," Harold said. "Tell me what you know. I'll tell you what I know. Perhaps together, we can find our way.

"I think we're both lost."

Chapter Twenty-Two

"I wish you were here with me, boy," Jeffrey said.

He crouched behind a tree, head poking out far enough for him to keep an eye on the two figures in the distance.

"How I wish you were with me." He could almost feel the dog's sturdy body, its warm fur beneath his arm, its encouraging licks to his face, its smiling, panting delight.

The auras of safety and contentment and belongingness had not begun when he had arrived in Elderton, Jeffrey now recognized. They had begun when he'd met the dog in the forest. Someday when he looked back, he would know that moment as the turning point in his life. A lost and lonely boy meeting a gloriously joyful dog in the midst of a dark forest.

If the dog had been by his side all along, maybe now he wouldn't be so terrified by the mere thought of sitting next to poor little Vida Proust in school, or by the memory of telling his new friend and roommate Bert Frehley that he was dead and then watching him fall to the hard, cold ground with such force it looked like he might shatter.

Maybe if the dog had been by his side, this moment he could calm himself enough to appreciate what he was seeing, and to decide what to do next.

It was scary enough to watch the dirty blind man shambling aimlessly through the forest. In and of itself, that sight had caused Jeffrey to throw himself down behind a tree and hide.

But then a strange little creature had clambered down from a treetop and walked right up to the blind man. It seemed like they had remained there for ages, talking.

Now the two were walking hand in hand into the distance, dusk gathering around them.

Jeffrey squinted and tried to make out what the small creature looked like. As best as he could tell, it was about three feet tall and perfectly proportioned, naked, and without a hair on its body. Its skin shone a soft lavender hue and it walked with a grace and ease that almost made it look like it was floating.

Taking in the unearthly scene, an understanding draped itself over Jeffrey Sprague. When he'd run away from the Presence Chamber after telling Bert he was dead, his supercharged body had insisted they were going somewhere. It was so sure of itself. Now, seeing the blind man and the little creature walking hand in hand, an important question forced itself on Jeffrey.

Where am I going?

Sure, he could return to the Keokuk foster home, although his absence likely worried the foster parents enough, and angered his caseworker enough, to make swift placement in yet another foster home all but certain.

I don't want that, Jeffrey thought. *I* won't *have that.*

In response to the question, it was as if his only friend—the nameless mutt—descended from heaven, pressed a big, loving tongue against his cheek, then whispered the answer in his ear.

Of course!

There was one other option. Even though the man had killed his dog, he had helped to bury him, too, so he wasn't all bad. And maybe his idea of taking Jeffrey to see a social worker was just a way he was trying to help out.

Ben Savitch didn't seem to fit into the Elderton Jeffrey had come to know. He wasn't like the other people Jeffrey had met since arriving. That was a promising thought; although everyone had been so nice to Jeffrey, perhaps he'd be a little safer around someone different. There had been something scary beneath all that niceness, anyway. He knew that now, after watching Bert die. And Miss Gayle: she'd brought the dead Bert to Jeffrey's side like nothing strange was going on at all. How could she have done that if she cared?

Yes. And Ben Savitch was a newspaper reporter, always interested in a story, just like the story of the crashed UFO. He knew what to do with facts, how to dig into a story and find the truth.

Perhaps they were the perfect match. Jeffrey had something to give the man: information. And perhaps in turn the man would allow Jeffrey the two things he most needed: sanctuary and understanding.

The sky was bruising, sunlight dwindling.

Jeffrey took one last look at the two retreating figures, then darted off in a different direction, running on tiptoes so the blind man and the tiny alien wouldn't hear him.

He'd find that guy, Ben Savitch. Then everything would be all right.

He hoped.

Chapter Twenty-Three

Ben rubbed his eyes for what seemed like the thousandth time since Audrey and he had started talking, as if a small part of him thought by doing so, everything would change, reality would assemble itself into the neat, straight little rows he'd always managed to impose upon it before. "So that article I read wasn't a hallucination, huh? This little girl, Vida Proust, she's dead? I mean, really dead?"

Audrey rolled down the car window and didn't turn back to answer the question, instead letting the rushing wind carry away her words. "Yes, she's dead."

Ben raked a hand through his hair. "Jesus, how did you . . . I don't know, put up with all of this without going crazy, or calling the FBI or something?"

"I'm not sure. I think when I arrived back in town, my mind and heart were full of expectations. I'd succeeded in my career and I'd already decided that the one thing missing from my life was a nest. I came here to nest, silly as that may sound to you. Everyone made me feel so welcome. There was such gentleness, caring, cooperation, that I guess I somehow found myself able to ignore the fact that Vida was dead by concentrating on the fact that it was the town's hope that was keeping her alive. I found poetry in that, and compared it to the poetry that was here when we were children. I fooled myself. I didn't see the whole picture. Things are different now. You can understand that, can't you?"

The sun was almost down. Ben clicked on his headlights and leaned closer to the steering wheel. He didn't want to miss the turn to Lou Bentley's farm.

Ben said, "And you lost that sense of beauty and poetry when that kid—"

"Yes, when Bert Frehley died. It was like a bucket of cold water was thrown in my face. Now I feel like such a fool, like somehow Bert would be alive if only I'd done something."

Ben couldn't resist. He reached over and patted Audrey's shoulder. What surprised him more was that it didn't even seem like a contrivance or just a means to an end. He felt something for this woman, something he hadn't felt in a long, long time. He didn't have a name for it, but wondered if it might be compassion.

Compassion equals pity minus condescension. Wasn't that what Almo had said? The equation fit.

"I can see why Elderton seduced you, Audrey. If I weren't such a cynical character, I'm sure it would've had the same effect on me. And you know something? Until you said it, I hadn't realized it . . . but I don't have a nest either. Just hearing you say that makes me wonder."

"About what?"

Ben shook his head. He wasn't sure he liked these new feelings. Sure there was warmth and fullness to them, but the accompanying uncertainty was a tad disquieting.

If Ben had achieved anything in his life, it was an unchanging illusion of certainty . . . even when he didn't have a clue what was going on.

"I don't know," he said, retreating into familiar emotional territory. "But now I can't decide whether I'm happy or not about not remembering my years here. It's like my life started when Mom and Dad and I moved to Chicago."

"You were a good boy, a happy boy, a funny boy," said Audrey. "I'm sure there would be plenty of nice things for you to remember. It's not like I'm saying Elderton is evil or anything. The old magic, the magic I remember, is still here. It's just that there's this other layer over it now."

Ben spied the familiar fenceline just ahead, the opening to Lou Bentley's farmland. He slowed the Civic, made the turn, and kept driving at a measured speed as the car entered by way of the faint dirt path.

As the Civic crested a tall hill, the setting sun came into view, red as a summer tomato, peeking through a tangled thicket of distant trees.

They were close.

Stopping and shutting off the engine, he unlatched his seat belt and turned to Audrey. "Tell me something. You remember me when we were kids. You remember a lot about Elderton. Do you remember Almo Parrish? I mean, it seems like if I would've remembered anyone it would have been a little guy who could predict a falling leaf and claimed he was in *The Wizard of Oz*."

Audrey pressed the knuckle of her index finger between her teeth. "You know something? I *do* remember Almo. But he wasn't the center of this town like he is now, not even close. He was just a little man who did odd jobs around town—mowing lawns in the summer, scooping snow off the sidewalks in the winter, cleaning out eaves in the fall and spring—someone everyone felt a little sorry for, someone everyone tried to look out for."

"So you don't remember the magic either?"

"Just the magic of a little town where people cared for one another, lifted one another up. Nothing that hurt anyone."

"How about this Presence Chamber you were telling me about?"

"I don't remember that either. It's an old building, and I think it used to be the dog pound. I can remember us going there when I was a girl and picking out a stray to take home."

"This is amazing," Ben said, leaning back in his seat and gazing through the windshield. "You were here with your family until you graduated from high school. Only twenty-five years ago or so. I wonder when things changed."

"I'm not sure," Audrey said.

"So you've never been in this Presence Chamber, the place where they take the blindfolded kids?"

"No. Almo promised I could go when it got closer to Christmas. He wanted to take me there personally."

"As a reporter, I think one thing I could do to try and unravel this story would be to . . . well, take a peek inside this Presence Chamber."

"You mean break in, I assume."

Ben forced a laugh. He'd felt them getting too somber over the past several minutes. "Hey you, I'm a professional. We don't do things like that. I would just, uh, gain entry, let's say."

Audrey smiled her beautiful smile and Ben felt his stomach fluttering nicely.

"Mind if I come with you?" she asked.

Ben opened the car door and stepped out. "Having a local resident with me when I . . . gain entry would be an excellent idea. But right now, we have something more important staring us in the face. Come on, Audrey Gayle. Let's go recover a crashed UFO."

She got out of the car and Ben helped her climb over the barbed wire fence surrounding Lou Bentley's pasture. When he touched her, he felt warm electricity shimmering through him.

She followed him down the gently sloping hill, through the flowing mass of tall prairie grass. Halfway down, she started to stumble and grabbed Ben's arm. Her hand then slid down and he linked his fingers with hers. They walked together in silence, Ben smiling more than he had since Darla left him.

"That's it?" Audrey exclaimed, pointing. "It's so small."

"I know, but that's the spacecraft. I looked inside it earlier. It even has a little seat."

"I wonder why it's still just sitting here."

Ben shrugged. "Maybe there's so much lunacy in this town that a disabled extraterrestrial spacecraft is several rungs down on the ladder of priorities."

They crept close to the craft, which lay bobbing back and forth with the rhythm of the languidly passing creek-water.

Ben touched the UFO, freshly amazed at the soft, velvety texture of its skin. Then, with Audrey gripping the back of his belt so he wouldn't fall into the water, he reached out with both hands and easily lifted the craft into the air.

"My God," Ben said, "it's as light as a balloon."

Ben carried the craft above his head as he walked back up the hill, Audrey behind him. When he reached the fenceline, he gently dropped the UFO to the other side. It took its sweet time dropping to the ground.

After helping Audrey over the fence, Ben again picked up the small UFO.

"What happens now?" Audrey asked.

"For now, we take this back to my motel room. Hell, it's so small and flexible we'll have no trouble getting it through the door. I can get a piece off of it, inform some top news brass of my find, get a camera crew sent down, and bust this story wide open. I'm not waiting on Almo and Chandler to reveal the secrets of Elderton. I'm wresting them out of their gnarled hands."

"I'm on your side. You deserve the story. You deserve to be as happy as I remember you, Benny."

He smiled at that. "Do you know the last time someone called me Benny?"

"No, when?"

"Beats the hell out of me." Well, maybe there was that one time, during the honeymoon with the comely contortionist Darla, when she'd worn a skin-tight leather bodysuit and barked decisive orders for him to—

"One more question, Benny. How do we get the UFO from here back to the motel room?"

"Simple. I set it on top of my trusty little car, we each stick an arm out the window and hold on to it, and I drive very slowly."

"Aren't you afraid someone will notice?"

"In Elderton, Illinois? Where a dead girl walks the streets without anyone even throwing a lazy glance her way? Where a bogus Munchkin poses with cardboard cutouts? Where a blind man accosts total strangers and forces them to guide him around town? I don't think anyone will notice a damned thing."

Chapter Twenty-Four

"Okay, Audrey, when I say three, give it one more good shove."

Standing just inside his motel room, Ben's face was squeezed into the side of the teardrop-shaped craft, its silky exterior pressing against his face, even invading his nostrils a bit. The craft was throbbing ever so slightly.

"Ready when you are, Ben," Audrey said. With the UFO halfway inside, completely filling the doorway, her voice sounded a block away.

"One . . . two . . ."

Ben was preparing to say "Three!"—the tip of his tongue pinched between his teeth—when he felt something brush the back of his leg and heard a voice say, "Mr. Savitch?"

Audrey's hearing must have been impaired as well, leading her to think Ben had given the cue, for just a second later the UFO squeezed through the doorway.

Ben took a step backward but it wasn't fast enough. Like a bar of soap escaping a wet fist, the UFO popped into the room.

Falling on his back, Ben's hands still clutched the craft as it sat atop him, pulsing.

Voice muffled, he said, "Get this thing offa me, Audrey! There's someone in the room! Help!"

Audrey calmly lifted the craft off of Ben and navigated it to the bed, where she gently set it down.

Ben whipped his head around, imagining that his room might have been invaded by anyone from the noxious Harold Brainard to the dead Vida Proust to the alien himself, who would be mighty torqued that his space wagon was now resting on a musty unmade bed in the PrairieView Motel, its nest a multitude of fanned-out *Peoria Journal-Star*s.

"Hi, Mr. Savitch. Ben." Jeffrey Sprague raised one hand in a sheepish wave.

"How did you get in here? What the hell are you—?"

Before Ben had a chance to finish, he heard Audrey gasp. "My goodness! Jeffrey!"

She ran to the boy, bent down and enfolded him in a big hug.

"Hi, Miss Gayle."

"Oh, Jeffrey," Audrey said, sounding like she was on the verge of sobbing, "I thought I'd never see you again."

There was no mistaking Jeffrey's reaction. He *was* sobbing, so hard he couldn't speak.

Audrey stepped back and laid her hand beneath Jeffrey's chin, first cradling it then tipping it up until their eyes met.

"Are you all right, Jeffrey? I've been so worried about you."

Ben watched the scene, unsure whether he should gather himself close to the two and join in, or just stand there and continue to feel envious that Jeffrey had received a big hug from the gorgeous Audrey.

He wasn't accustomed to situations like this. The last time he remembered high emotion appearing in a personal relationship was the night Darla had thrown a crock pot at him after he'd made a relatively innocuous remark about her mother's physical attributes.

Audrey led Jeffrey to the bed—casually shoving aside the UFO as if it were nothing more important than a decoration they'd picked up at the dime store—then sat down next to the boy.

"Now, tell me, where have you been?" Audrey said, laying an arm across Jeffrey's shoulders. "You had me worried sick."

Jeffrey sniffed several times, ran an arm across his nose.

Ben went into the bathroom and yanked the last three Kleenexes out of the box, took them back in, and handed them to the crying boy.

There. I'm being productive.

"When Bert came and I saw what happened to him—"

Audrey pulled his head to her breast, saying, "I know, I know."

"I got so scared I just couldn't stay any more. But then I figured out that I didn't have no place else to go. I thought maybe Mr. Savitch could help me."

"Yeah?" Ben said, walking closer to the two, excited that he might not remain excluded. "How do you think I might help you?"

Jeffrey blew his nose in a piercing A-flat. "I thought maybe if I told you what I saw, you'd help me, protect me."

"What did you see?" asked Ben.

"I think I saw the alien you were lookin' for."

Ben sat down beside Jeffrey. Although he didn't remember if he'd ever done something like this before, he too laid a hand across Jeffrey's shoulders, as much to graze Audrey's arm as to comfort the kid.

"What did the alien look like?"

"He was real short and he didn't have any hair on him and his skin shined kinda purple."

"What was he doing?" Ben asked.

"He was talking to a blind man."

Ben raised his head toward the ceiling and winced.

Harold Brainard again. God, just in case You're wondering, that offer about walloping me with the piano still stands.

Audrey bent forward to get Ben in her eyeline. "We've got to do something, Ben."

Ben stood up and could almost feel the testosterone boiling through his innards. He was being directly invited to be the man of the house, as it were. Placing his hands on his hips, he thrust out his chest and stuck out his lower lip.

A second later he softened his stance a bit, realizing he was effecting a dead-on impression of Barney Fife.

Raising an index finger into the air, Ben said, "Okay. Here's what we're going to do. Johnny—"

"Jeffrey."

"Jeffrey, you and Audrey, you're going to stay here. You'll be nice and safe. You can keep an eye on the UFO for me."

"Where are you going?" Audrey asked.

He turned around quickly to face her. "I'm going to march right down to Almo Parrish's house . . . well, drive, actually."

"You're going to confront Almo?"

"You bet I am. Just watch me."

His movements still felt stiff and Knotts-like but he didn't care anymore. He was getting into this. By confronting the last Munchkin—whoever and whatever the hell he was—Ben could get his story by wringing it out of the little man, protect the little kid whose dog he'd hit, and perhaps wipe one little smudge off the cosmic blackboard that displayed slash-marks representing all of his earthly screw-ups.

And—who knew—maybe he'd even get the girl.

Chapter Twenty-Five

"How dare you barge into my home and threaten me?" Almo said it in a stern voice, but his lips—as well as his little body—were quivering.

"I didn't barge in," Ben said, poised in the front doorway with his arms crossed in front of him like James Dean . . . or a drunken Barney Fife. "I knocked, all right? I came over here because whatever freaky stuff is happening here has got to stop. Now! Tonight I saw a little boy crying, scared out of his wits because of the stuff he's seen in this town. Tonight Audrey and I talked. My God, Almo, she came back to Elderton for a little peace and belongingness, not so she could play taxi driver to a dead kid!"

Ben was slamming into overdrive. It felt so good. Once he'd started, he'd just let it all gush out: all the frustrations he'd experienced these years, all the pent-up rage at being rejected and scoffed at. He was letting it all pour out and drench the last Munchkin and it felt so damned good.

"I didn't have anything to do with that boy dying," Almo said, backing up into his living room. "You know that. You know I'd never—"

"What I *do* know is that you're the core of this Twilight Zone, and the weirdness is scaring and hurting people. If you don't mind me saying, Almo, kids dying ain't good magic."

Almo backed up farther, then sat down on the couch and laid his hands in his lap. He bowed his head. "Chandler was right," he whispered. "You're the invader. You're the one who's come to destroy our town."

152

Ben stomped the rest of the way into the house. "Don't you try to pin this shit on me, Almo! I'm destroying nothing. You can't pull the stuff on me that you can pull on everyone else. For example . . ." He walked over and picked up the photo from the old TV set. "This picture is total bullshit! I happen to know that you're not the last Munchkin. Hell, you're no Munchkin at all! I've met some Munchkins, and you aren't one of them. You're not even short enough. And this picture . . ."

He tossed it and it landed on Almo's lap. Almo picked it up, blew dust off it, and stared at the photograph as he cradled the frame.

"That's not Judy Garland, Almo. I don't know who you think you're dealing with, but it's clear as the hair growing out of your ears. Just look at the reflections in the picture."

Almo was looking.

"That's not a human being you're posing with. That's a goddamned cardboard cutout!"

"What?" Almo said, his voice puzzled and wispy. "But I thought—"

"Oh, come off it, Almo! Look at me! Look . . . at . . . me!"

Almo brought his eyes up to meet Ben's. Tears pooled in them.

"I didn't just fall off the back of one of your blindfolded-children-carrying pickup trucks, you know. I've been married and divorced three times. I've had—hell, I don't know—twenty jobs in my career. I can't be easily fooled."

"Fascinating," Almo said, wiping his eyes and almost smiling.

"What's fascinating?"

"It sounds like you tally the score of your life by counting the number of things you've turned away from."

"Don't give me that crap!" Ben spat. "Just tell me where the alien is, Almo."

"That's what this is about for you? The alien? The story? Making a name for yourself? Pulling one over on the town that nourished you when you were a baby?"

"Yes, that's exactly right. That, and putting a stop to the psychotic, sadistic magic you're responsible for."

"I don't know where the alien is."

"You *are* a worthless little pile of Munchkin dung, aren't you?"

Ben whirled around and marched toward the open front door.

He'd done what he could do here and, by now, he was so pumped with anger that he knew that if he remained a second longer the next thing he'd do would be to beat the last Munchkin down to pillow-mint size, resulting in having himself thrown in the local jail where they likely taught people manners by plucking out their nostril hairs one by one in some kind of arcane ritual of nasal soul cleansing.

When he blurred through the doorway, it felt like he walked full speed into a brick wall. Ben fell flat on his back then looked up, fists clenched, vision sparkling, ready to take on anyone crazy enough to cross his path. He was *that* pumped.

What he saw gave him pause. It was Frank Shepard, standing there with the biggest grin on his face. And there was something wrong, either with Ben's vision or with Frank himself. He was flickering. The edges of his body seemed fringed with tiny multicolored flames, wavering and lapping and fading.

Chandler poked his head out from behind the reanimated Sky-Lord.

"Sorry about that, young Ben. Frank here doesn't know his strength yet, it seems."

Frank kept smiling as he reached up and adjusted his glasses.

Wrinkling his brow, Frank asked, "Is this man a villain, Mr. Quinn?"

Patting Frank on the shoulder, Chandler said with a laugh, "Oh, no. This is an ally, my befuddled god-man."

"Wait just a minute there," Almo called from the living room couch. "He just came over here to threaten me, Chandler."

Chandler pushed Frank aside. Then, as he reached down to help Ben to his feet, he said, "What is this he's telling me? Menacing Almo, the last Munchkin? Tell me that my petite humanoid friend had misconstrued your intent."

"Spare me your Roget's Diarrhea, Chandler," Ben said, shoving his way past him. He nodded sternly to a still smiling Frank Shepard as he passed, then strode down the steps and into Almo's front yard.

The first thing he saw was Vida Proust stumbling by on the sidewalk. Still feverish with anger and frustration, Ben said, "Come out here, both of you!"

Almo and Chandler appeared at the door, standing abreast of Frank Shepard.

Ben pointed to Vida. "You see that? You call that good magic? My God, Almo, I happen to know that little girl fell into a well and died three weeks ago!"

Simultaneously, Almo and Chandler gasped. Their faces turned the color of dust. Almo clapped a hand to his mouth like he might vomit.

Vida stopped, turned, and stood there, arms hanging limply at her sides. Her face was blank, but within those glassy eyes Ben noticed something.

Fear. Horror. Dread. Something.

She turned back to continue walking, as if she wanted to forget what she'd heard. But something was different. Before, her movements were stiff and jerky. Now it looked as if she were turning to ice, her steps punctuated by weak, grotesque spasms. So slow.

No one said a word.

The four of them watched as Vida Proust struggled so hard, so excruciatingly slowly, to plod her way down the sidewalk, to get out of earshot of the man who had just told her she was dead. It took her several minutes to walk ten feet, until the shrubs surrounding the adjacent home obscured her.

Turning again to face the three men on the front stoop, Ben held out his hands, palms up. "I didn't know—"

In the blink of an eye, Frank was standing right in front of him, smiling grimly, shaking his head back and forth.

"You hurt a little girl," Frank said. "You *are* a villain."

Still reeling from the fact that the Frank Shepard lookalike had seemingly traversed twenty feet of ground in less than a second, Ben couldn't respond.

Frank grabbed Ben's lapels tightly and lifted him into the air.

"Frank?" Chandler called. "Perchance you shouldn't—"

Before Chandler could complete his sentence, Frank had hoisted Ben above his head like he was a fleshy spear, turned around, and launched him.

Ben heard himself screaming as he sailed through the cool night air. He landed hard on the roof of Almo's house, the rough shingles scraping both arms, then grabbed the top of a gable so he wouldn't fall the twenty feet to the ground.

He carefully turned over.

Frank stood below him, looking up with that same

156

knowing grin on his face. Then he took off his wire-rimmed glasses, narrowed his eyes, and stared menacingly at Ben.

Twin streaks of lightning discharged from Frank's eyes.

Immediately Ben felt his feet burning. The soles of his shoes burst into fire.

"My God!" he cried, reaching down and patting away the flames. "Owwww!"

Frank took two steps, bounced once on the ground, extended his fists, and flew to the rooftop, gracefully landing next to Ben.

He stood over Ben and said with a smirk, "Maybe you should think twice before you hurt a little girl."

Chapter Twenty-Six

By the time he returned to his room at the PrairieView, Ben had nearly thrust the image of the shambling Vida Proust out of his mind, fixating instead on the fact that now he was even more certain that Elderton's magic was destructive.

He had the chafed arms and scorched feet to prove it.

Also, he now believed that Frank Shepard was indeed Frank Shepard and not just a look-alike from a local Men's Goods department. Being assaulted with superhuman powers had a way of addressing skepticism.

As he pushed his key into the door to unlock it, it swung open.

Audrey and Jeffrey were sitting on the bed, watching an old black-and-white movie on the television. Quite a sight— two people calmly enjoying a movie while an alien craft sat pulsing on the floor next to the bed, clear as day.

Audrey looked concerned. "Did everything go okay?"

Before Ben could answer, Jeffrey curled his nose and asked, "What's that smell?"

Ben picked up his foot from the floor and displayed the melted sole of his shoe. "One of Almo's friends set fire to me."

"You're kidding," Audrey said, getting up and walking to Ben.

"It's okay. I'm okay."

She touched his shoulder. "You're sure?"

"I'm sure. Jeffrey, if Audrey and I are gone for a while, will you be okay?"

Jeffrey had kicked back, now lying on the bed with pillows

stuffed behind his head. He barely glanced over. "I'll be fine. I feel good again. Safe. We've been watching television and I've been looking through some of your newspapers. They were interesting."

"Then come with me, Audrey. We've got one more trip to take tonight."

"Where?"

"The Presence Chamber."

That got Jeffrey's attention. "Can I come?"

"No, pal, you stay here. We don't know what we're going to find out there."

Jeffrey seemed vaguely disappointed, but recovered quickly and became reabsorbed in the movie.

Ben scrabbled through his overnight bag and extracted a pair of tattered white Keds. He started to throw away the roasted shoes, then thought better of it. A nice sidebar to his Elderton story. He'd save them for further evidence:

REPORTER ASSAULTED
BY REANIMATED TELEVISION SUPERHERO

He slipped on the Keds and joined Audrey.

After they walked outside, Ben checked the door twice to ensure it was locked.

"Oh, I almost forgot," Audrey said. "The motel office called. They said they have a message for you from earlier today. From a Max somebody."

Ben huffed. "Max Thomason. Television anchor in Chicago and someone who I thought respected my judgment. We're old friends. But I told him everything that was happening down here and he laughed it off. Screw him."

"You don't want the message?"

"I'll pick it up later. This is more important now."

Audrey guided Ben as he drove to the Presence Chamber.

He didn't want to ask, but the image had returned. As much as he wanted to, he couldn't just let it sit. "Audrey, you know that girl, Vida Proust?"

"Of course."

"I know she's alive because no one will tell her she's dead. What would happen . . . if someone did tell her?"

"The same thing that happened to Bert Frehley, I guess. She'd die."

Today, as it turned out, was a day of new feelings all the way around. Ben had felt honest compassion toward Audrey, stirrings of attraction for Audrey, traces of pity for Jeffrey, and now . . .

What was that feeling?

Like a thick hot spike drilling through his guts.

Guilt, maybe?

It was hard to say. It had been so long. In fact, he wasn't sure he'd ever felt it before.

Moments of silence passed, then Audrey said, "Why do you ask?"

"Ask what?"

"About Vida."

Ben hesitated. Up until now, it had seemed like things were going so smoothly between Audrey and him that she had begun to regard him with some respect and, yes, perhaps even a little affection.

He finally said, "Promise you won't hate me?"

She didn't respond.

Ben sighed deeply, unconsciously flicking on his headlights as he drove down a winding gravel road. "I was pretty mad at Almo and Chandler and when I left Almo's house, Vida was walking by."

"Yes?"

160

"Well . . . I yelled something to Almo about her being dead . . . and she heard me."

"Oh my God. What happened?"

"She stopped for a second, then she walked away. But she was walking slower, like she could barely move her legs."

"Oh my God," Audrey repeated.

Ben couldn't think of anything else to say. Did a person apologize for pointing out that a dead person is dead? Was that considered a violation of otherworldly etiquette?

But he knew: Audrey cared for the girl, had her in class. No matter whether she was alive or dead, Audrey had been a loving guardian for Vida Proust.

For a moment Ben considered the fact that he had now witnessed more paranormal events during his brief stay in Elderton than he had during the balance of his life, and wondered why it hadn't shaken him more or encouraged at least a tiny sense of awe. Perhaps there were advantages to being a cynic; even true magic seemed like nothing more special than advanced parlor tricks. What was the old saying? A cynic is a person who knows the cost of everything and the value of nothing? Perhaps there was truth to that. And perhaps, in this situation, Ben's sardonic outlook was a gift.

Audrey started to say something, but only an "uh" came out. She paused, then tried again: "Maybe . . . maybe that's for the best."

"Yeah. Maybe." But he'd heard the disbelief in her tone.

"Here it is, Ben. Right up here."

He turned into a large circular gravel driveway surrounding a small tumble-down brick building.

He wanted to leave the topic of Vida Proust behind for good, although he didn't know if that were possible. It was worthy of a try, so he focused on the task at hand.

"Let me get some tools out of the trunk and we'll go in."

"Sure," Audrey said absently. "That will be fine."

He popped open the trunk lid and dug through the contents of his large toolbox, finding a hammer and a large pipe wrench. Just to be on the safe side, he grabbed the jack, too.

Audrey stood beneath the warm golden light at the front entrance of the building.

"I think I can get us in," Ben said, brandishing the tools. He noticed that his voice wasn't nearly as testosterone-saturated as it had been earlier.

Perhaps killing a little dead girl did that to you.

Audrey turned toward the door, then said, "I don't think that will be necessary."

She pushed, and the door swung open.

"I'll be damned," Ben said, "you rural people really *don't* lock your doors."

Ben pushed open the door the rest of the way, setting down his tools just inside.

The building was a symphony of smells: old wax, old paper, old dogs. Old life.

"Strange. You said that this used to be the dog pound. I can still smell the dogs."

"Me, too."

He found a light switch on one wall and flipped it up. The large, open central room was a mess. It looked like no one had cleaned the place in decades. Cobweb architecture was the most symmetrical facet of the furnishings, long flowing meshes draping every corner.

Chairs were overturned on the floor. Crushed Styrofoam coffee cups littered the area, as did innumerable cigarette butts.

"This is some kind of holy place?" Ben said. "Jeez.

162

Looks more like a bus station bathroom."

Audrey didn't respond. She wandered over to one side of the room, where at least ten large Army-green filing cabinets—most of them dented and rust-spotted—stood in a line like drunken soldiers, pitching this way and that.

"Look, Ben. Look at these."

He stood beside her, looking closely at the file cabinets. Hastily scribbled labels were pasted to each drawer.

Ben said, "There are years listed on each drawer."

Scanning the cabinets, Audrey said, "You're right. All the years from 1950 until this year."

"Great," Ben said. "Maybe there are records, documents to explain what the hell's going on around here. That makes sense. They bring the kids out, explain the true nature of Elderton, then threaten to kill them if they ever say a word about it. The kids are recruited into some kind of loose, loony cult."

Audrey was hardly paying attention, walking up and down the queue of cabinets until she finally located a drawer reading "1967." When she yanked it open, it screeched and cawed as if she were torturing it.

"Why 1967?" Ben asked.

She shrugged. "I was just trying to think of a year that would have some meaning to me, someplace to start; 1967 was the year Dad died."

"I'm sorry."

"Long time ago."

He looked over her shoulder as she scrutinized the drawer's contents.

Rather than being stuffed full of files, it looked to be packed with opaque plastic sandwich bags, haphazardly arranged behind battered, multi-colored dividers. Hundreds of them.

Audrey flipped past the dividers until she reached "G." She pulled out two handfuls of the bags.

"Each one is labeled," she said.

Just as she'd said, each plastic bag sported a small note with messy writing taped to its front.

"What do they say?"

"Names," Audrey said, "names of townspeople. And dates."

"Find anything belonging to anybody you know?"

Audrey gasped. "I don't believe this."

She held up the bag for him to see.

The note read: "Seth Aaron Gayle. June 3, 1967."

"That's my dad," Audrey whispered.

She carefully opened the bag, reached in slowly, and pulled out a scrap of cloth that was folded into a four-inch square. It was thick brown fabric, tattered and nondescript, with a plaid pattern, one button sewed to it.

Audrey frowned. "What could this be?"

"You don't recognize it?"

She shook her head, turned over the cloth several times then finally, as if she could think of nothing else to do with it, pressed it to her face and inhaled deeply.

The effect was instantaneous. Moaning, she fell backward.

Ben caught her. Had she fainted?

He lowered her carefully to the floor.

"Audrey. What's wrong?"

Cloth still pressed to her face, she said, "Oh, Ben. I can smell him. I can smell Dad. I can smell his Old Spice and his pipe tobacco and the bratwurst he used to burn on the grill. I can smell mown grass and sweet ground coffee and the horehound drops he liked. I can smell *him*."

She began to weep.

Ben knelt behind her and held her close.

"It's like he's right here with me," she said, unfolding the cloth and covering her entire face. "Ben, it's like he's right here with me."

Chapter Twenty-Seven

They pulled into the parking lot of the PrairieView, Audrey only now collecting herself. She stared at the floor of the car, mesmerized, hands clasped in front of her, eyes wide, breathing deeply as if she were still smelling the swath of her father's suit coat she'd found at the Presence Chamber.

Ben switched off the engine and touched her on the shoulder. "Are you okay now, Audrey?"

Emerging from her reverie, she nodded, then daubed at her nose with a handkerchief. "You see what it is now? The Presence Chamber? It's a place they take the kids to immerse them in the town by immersing them in others. It's a way to never forget what's here . . . to never forget what's most important. They can take the children out there, let them smell the belongings of people who are long gone, or those who have grown old, and give them a sense of who's been here, past and present. They can smell belongings of their own and remember a summer day or a birthday party or a vacation. They can recall and connect. There's something quite beautiful about it all."

"Why fabric? Each of those bags had cloth in them. Why not just have—I don't know—a photo gallery or something?"

"Ben, all I can say is my experience out there was much more powerful than looking at photos of Dad would have been. It brought back a rush of memories, sounds, emotions, everything."

Ben opened his car door. "Why don't you go on in and see how Jeffrey's doing? I'll stop by the motel office and

166

pick up that message they said was waiting for me."

She nodded again, still preoccupied by thought or emotion or memory.

Ben jammed his hands into his pockets as he walked past the row of motel rooms. The only thing distinguishing the office from the other rooms was a sign taped to the door reading OFFICE, the C written backward.

He knocked.

"Yes, come right in," a voice sang.

Opening the door, the beaming face of an overweight middle-aged woman greeted him. Her coal-black hair was fashioned into a chic helmet-like coiffure, and her face was made up like she might have been planning to attend the prom. "Hi, there. My name's Sophie Ardell, I work the night shift here."

She stood up from behind the counter and shook Ben's hand.

"Pleased," Ben said. "I'm Ben Savitch—"

"I know. I'm happy you came back to town. I always thought you and your family were wonderful, and I was worried we'd never see you again. Where are your folks these days?"

Of course, Ben had no memory of Sophie Ardell. "Mom's dead," Ben replied. "Dad's in a nursing home up north."

"I'm sorry to hear that. They were good people and you were such a good little boy."

"Thanks."

"I'm happy you came by. It gets kind of lonely here at night, as you might imagine."

"You had a message for me." The last thing he wanted was to get sucked into an interminable conversation with an understimulated local. "So do you have it?"

She lifted up a pair of reading glasses, which hung from a string of faux pearls around her neck. Perching them at the tip of her nose, she sat down and fingered her way through a small pile of pink notes scattered across her desk. "Have you made friends with Almo since returning?" she asked as she inspected each note with excessive care.

"Well . . . I guess so."

"I just wondered. I was looking out the window earlier and saw him coming to visit you."

That took Ben by surprise. "When was that?"

"Hmm," she said, holding up one of the notes to the light as if she were analyzing a lab specimen. "A half hour or so ago. I probably made a note of it in my log if you want me to look it up. I keep track of things like that, just to keep myself occupied. Do you need specific information?"

"No. Just let me see my message."

She shot him a quick glance.

"Please?"

"That's better," Sophie said.

Why the hell would Almo Parrish come to my room, especially after the ugly scene tonight?

To abduct Jeffrey? To convince Audrey to turn against Ben? Or just to apply some kind of bogus Munchkin sorcery to the nosy and unsupportive Ben Savitch?

"Ah, here it is," she said, a smile stretching across her face, breaching sections of her pancake makeup. She held it out to Ben. "Here you go, Mr. Savitch. Benny."

Ben snatched the note from her hand, startling her.

"Thanks a lot," he said, turned and walked outside.

The night was growing teeth, an arresting tinge of ice joining the breeze. He pulled his collar tight around his neck with one hand as he unfolded the note with his other.

168

7:30 pm—Ben Savitch. Room 23
Max Thomason called. An old friend.
On his way down to see you.
Bringing a crew. Think of it as a special gift.
Welcome home, Benny Savitch.
THANK YOU FOR CHOOSING THE
PRAIRIEVIEW MOTEL, YOU LOVELY HUMAN

"Aha!" Ben said. "Maxipad finally saw the light."

He crumpled the note and threw it to the ground, then hurried to Room 23.

He wasn't surprised to find the door unlocked.

He *was* surprised by what he saw when he stepped inside.

The UFO was still resting on the floor in a corner.

Jeffrey seemed safe and sound, although the troubled look in his eyes gave Ben pause.

What was dumbfounding was to see Almo Parrish lying on the bed, his breath coming in ragged gasps, his face gone the color of a storm cloud.

Audrey sat next to him, holding a washcloth to his forehead.

"What's going on here?" Ben asked.

Audrey turned, eyes shimmering with tears, and shrugged.

The last Munchkin grunted as he forced his eyes half-open and turned them in Ben's direction. "I came . . . I came to apologize to you . . . Ben. I'm sorry about what happened tonight. You were right, Ben. Right."

Ben stepped closer. "What are you talking about?"

Almo coughed violently, raising his little body off the bed like he might levitate. "I didn't realize . . . I didn't know . . . I thought I knew Judy Garland . . . I thought I was a Munchkin . . . I couldn't remember the day the picture was taken . . . I guess the people in town were just doing me a favor, being nice to me . . . They've always been so nice to me . . . I couldn't remember anything at all before . . . before . . ."

"Before what?"

Almo raised a trembling hand and pointed to a newspaper scattered next to the bed. Then he seemed to lose all energy, sinking down into the mattress with an emptying sigh and closing his eyes.

Audrey continued wiping his forehead.

Jeffrey reached down, gathered up the newspaper and handed it to Ben.

It was a copy of the *Peoria Journal-Star* dated March 15, 1977. At the bottom of page two was the following story:

Elderton, Illinois—Two Elderton residents lost their lives last evening after a fiery explosion consumed the car in which they were riding. Both 55-year-old Almo Parrish and 43-year-old Chandler Quinn were killed when their car unexpectedly exploded.

Chandler Quinn, an Elderton attorney, was also an amateur inventor, according to Elderton Police Chief Joshua Huls. "He apparently had rigged up some kind of device that was supposed to save gas or something," Huls said. "That's what caused the explosion, as far as we can tell."

Prompt action on the part of the Elderton Emergency Medical Team and Elderton Volunteer Fire Department was unsuccessful in saving either man's life.

"The explosion blew them both plumb out of the car," Chief Huls continued. "Chandler ended up on Mayor Huston's front porch and Almo, he was found on the front lawn of the local high school. Such a tragedy."

Both men were beloved in their community, being known for their quiet kindness and generosity.

"It's a crying shame," said local resident Patty Penworth. "They were such dreamers . . ."

Time suspended, bubbles in amber. It seemed to take hours for Ben to drop the paper to the floor and raise his head.

He noticed the palm of Almo's left hand. It was darkening, shriveling, blistering.

"You've got to save him, Mr. Savitch," Jeffrey said, eyes imploring. "You've got to do something. He's dying."

Chapter Twenty-Eight

"Good God, aren't there any interstates in downstate Illinois?" Max Thomason flipped down the visor on the passenger side of the van, turned on the interior light, and checked his hair. Yes, every last silvery wave was in place.

"Not in this area of the state," replied his driver/cameraman, Wally Fesler. "They call West-Central Illinois Forgottonia, because it's like it's been forgotten. They even forgot to put in good roads down here."

"Primitive, so primitive. I hope it's worth it."

"Me, too, Max."

Max flipped off the light and sat back in his seat. "I'm banking on the fact that my story instincts are as strong as ever. When I last talked to him, Ben sparked an idea for me. With sweeps week just around the corner, it was worthy of consideration."

"You mean about the crashed UFO? You don't really believe that, do you?"

Max roared with laughter. "No, of course not. I mean, Ben's the guy who called me breathlessly to tell me he'd stumbled upon a tribe of fairy creatures who had been coming to Fairbury, Illinois, for some kind of annual memorial festival for all the dead fairies. Get it? Fair-bury? He claimed he'd arranged with a local optometrist to get the fairies together for group photos."

"Amazing. So he's pretty gullible."

"Gullible, but in an odd, pessimistic sort of way, Wally. You'd think someone who would spend days chasing down stories about paranormal phenomena would be an optimistic, spiritual sort. Not Ben. He's the most cynical, sardonic person I know. For him, I think he saw the stories as promising money, fame, power. He wanted those things so much he could convince himself the stories were true, for a little while at least. I guess you'd say he's a hopeful romantic, but in the most twisted sort of way."

"You sketch an interesting portrait of this guy."

"That's the point," Max said. "We can't lose. We'll get a story any way you look at it. If the one in a million is true and there *is* a crashed UFO, Ben will be only too willing to share every shred of information with us to get his face on television or get the elusive job offer he always thinks is just around the next corner. But more likely, he's chasing a mist again, which gives us a nice angle on tabloid newspapers, how ridiculous they are, how grizzled and credulous their reporters are. That's the secret of sweeps week, isn't it? Presenting a tabloid story without appearing to be tabloidish yourself? I figure we can follow him around as he goes on this wild goose chase. He might look a little lame in the process, but if his face gets on television, he won't even notice. Or even if he does, he won't care."

"Sounds like a good plan," Wally said.

"That's not all of it, either. I think we can squeeze a weeklong series out of this. At the very least, I thought it was a deserving enough venture to get this little convoy together. We all need to get out of the city sometimes, all of us, see what makes the rural folk tick. Or something like that. I even called some of our lesser regional affiliates to join us. If nothing else, we can have a nice party for a couple of days without the newsroom pressure, galvanize the relationships among the news crews. You never know when they'll come in handy for us. I convinced the station to pick up our lodging and meals and alcohol. I think everyone will have a great time."

"A nice idea, Max. I'm sure everybody appreciates it."

"And the series: we get a whole week's worth of stories, douse ourselves completely in the tabloid cesspool, and stay smelling as sweet as the perfume on a bowling alley prostitute's thighs."

"Brilliant."

"Are we almost there?"

"We're only five miles away."

"Great," Max said, linking his hands over his chest and closing his eyes. "Won't Ben be surprised. I hope he realizes what a favor I'm doing for him . . . even if he doesn't understand that he's the primary butt of the story. It never ceases to amaze me that someone who attended Columbia could be such a dip."

Chapter Twenty-Nine

Some would say I've ruined my share of lives in the past. Some would say I haven't even done a bad job on my own. But at least I've never really killed anyone.

Until I returned to Elderton.

The Vida Proust situation was bad enough, but now Almo.

Jesus.

Ben shook his head, tossing away the disturbing thought like yesterday's hot dog wrapper. Hell, Almo had simply read an article detailing his own death. Ben didn't have anything to do with it. Not a thing.

Nothing.

And Vida? Good Lord, the newspaper article clearly spelled out the fact that she'd been dead for three weeks.

Vida finding out she's dead was a blessing. Yeah. Her parents can now put her to rest and get on with their lives. Right. A favor. In the long run, I was doing good.

Almo's breathing was labored and shallow. Audrey had stopped stroking him with the washcloth, instead saturating it with cold water and laying it across his forehead.

Holding Almo's hand tightly with both of hers, she carefully watched the last Munchkin's chest as it rose and fell. A few times when it fell it looked like it might not rise again.

Jeffrey stood up and walked to Ben. He scuffed one shoe against the floor, hesitant. Then he asked, "You told Vida she was dead?"

"Well . . . yeah. I didn't mean to, not exactly. I was just—" He let it go. It wouldn't matter what he said. All he

175

knew was that because of him, this little boy thought there was a little girl dead somewhere in town, and a helpless old man lying in the bed two steps from the grave. Ben knew, without asking, that Jeffrey regarded him as a serial killer. In the filing cabinet of his mind, there wasn't anyplace to put experiences like this. Not even close. People dead and dying because of Ben Savitch. Even if it were a crazy thought and not really valid at all, it was unnerving to realize that's what the boy thought.

"Are you going to help Mr. Parrish?" Jeffrey asked.

"I don't know how to."

"If you can't help him, will you bury him like you did my dog?"

Just then, there was a horrible crash outside.

The way my luck's going, a B-52 probably just plummeted from the sky and landed on my Civic.

Ben opened the door.

It looked like a Fourth of July celebration.

A fountain of orange and red sparks sprayed heavenward from the big neon-covered PRAIRIEVIEW MOTEL sign. A large dent ruined its center, as if the sign had been struck by a meteorite.

Ben stepped outside, closed the door behind him. Whatever he found out there, after this night he doubted it would surprise him.

Noticing movement in the bushes surrounding the base of the sign, Ben walked closer.

Suddenly the air was filled with the booming, histrionic voice of Chandler Quinn: "I told you your aerial adroitness was yet to fully ripen! I should never have sanctioned you to give me a lift out here. My Rambler would have delivered us in better shape!"

Chandler rose to his feet, his gray ponytail pulled loose,

mustache lopsided, his clothes twisted to one side and half-unbuttoned.

Next, Frank Shepard got up, shaking his head as he straightened his wire-rimmed glasses. The damned guy was still blurry. Even more than the last time Ben had seen him which, come to think of it, was on the top of Almo's roof right after his shoes had erupted into flames.

It wasn't an hallucination after all. It was Frank Shepard. He's flickering like a candle ready to go out, like a spreading inkspot on paper. Leaking.

"Sorry, Mr. Quinn," Frank said, sympathetically patting his benefactor on the shoulder. "It won't happen again."

Noticing Ben, Chandler's face broke into a grin. "Say there, Ben Savitch! Just the gent I was searching for. I hear that Almo came out to pay you a visit. Has he arrived?"

"Uh . . . yes." *Talk about a forgiving nature. Not long ago I invaded Almo's house, insulted everything these guys stand for, and informed Vida Proust that she was a walking cadaver. Now he's treating me like a favored nephew.*

"Wonderful wonderful wonderful. Did you see me and my flying crony make our detonating ingress? It was something! Thank goodness I wasn't maimed. Frank here . . . well, I guess he had little to worry about, being invulnerable, insubstantial, all that. Am I correct, Frank of the Mangled Sign?"

"Again, I'm so sorry, Mr. Quinn," Frank said, his voice crackling, sounding distant. "And to you, too, Mr. Savitch. I'm sorry about being a little rough with you tonight. I didn't understand the situation, I guess. I get confused easily."

"It's okay," Ben said. "Don't worry about it."

Chandler stage-whispered, "You'll have to excuse Frank. He's depressed. He feels himself fading and believes he isn't

177

contributing what he'd like to the world."

Frank shrugged. "I'm not going to be here long. I want to make a difference. I want to be a hero, just once, before I go."

Chandler nodded, a trace of pity shading his face. "Yes, yes. And now, Ben, about Almo?"

"He's in my room."

Chandler grabbed Frank by the arm and started for Room 23.

Suddenly it struck Ben. "Wait!"

"Yes, my dear boy?"

What the hell was he going to say? That Almo was withering away in the motel room because he had died twenty years ago in a car wreck with Chandler, who had also died, toasted crispier than a corn chip?

He had to think. The situation was becoming more desperate, more insanely immediate, with each passing moment.

Coming up dry from the well of ideas, he finally said, "He's sleeping in there. He's not feeling well."

"Don't worry. My flickering friend and I shall not disturb the Munchkin's slumber."

As hard as he tried, Ben couldn't think of anything else to add. "Go on in then. The door's open."

Chandler and Frank disappeared into the motel room. Ben didn't want to imagine what would be happening in there during the next hour.

He paced the motel's parking lot, which was abandoned save for his Civic, Audrey's Camry, and glittering shards of glass from the ruined sign. Maybe the crisp air would wake him up, clear his head, innervate his thought processes.

Reaching a corner of the one-story structure, he turned, heading out back. The PrairieView was situated in front of an immense cornfield, no other buildings nearby. Perhaps a nice hike through a half-dead cornfield would be good for the soul. At least it would get him away from the people, the noise, the emotion. Away from Room 23.

Only a few stray lights illuminated the rear of the motel, making it difficult to see. Ben sat down against a wall, pulled his knees up, and wrapped his arms around them.

All these years, he'd asked for a situation like this, something so dramatic, so fantastic that his reportage would electrify not only the public, but the journalistic world. And didn't he have enough already, for God's sake? He not only owned a chunk of the UFO, he had the whole damned thing sitting in his motel room, throbbing like a weak heart.

Hell, if I only had the alien, I'd be hosting the "Ben Savitch News Cavalcade Power Hour" before I knew it.

He had begun sorting out the situation, sifting his priorities, when a chilling voice sliced the night's silence.

"Help us," the voice said. It was a weak voice. And familiar.

Ben squinted.

Above the drooping cornstalks he made out a head bobbing toward him, a head covered with poorly cut, greasy dark hair.

"Someone's there?" the voice asked, its source approaching.

What the hell?

Caution be damned at this point, Ben called, "Yeah, come on over, whoever you are. Might as well join the party."

Harold Brainard emerged from the cornfield and—just as Jeffrey Sprague had described—the blind man was walking hand-in-hand with a tiny figure.

Ben stood. "Is that the alien?" It was like God or some

other large entity had heard his needs and immediately dispatched the answer by special delivery.

Here's your alien, Benny-boy. Have a rollicking good time as you revel in your fame and fortune. You don't even need to thank me. You deserve it, buddy.

"Is that you?" Harold Brainard said, breaking into his gap-toothed smile. "I remember walking with you."

"Yeah, I won't forget that either." He tried to maintain his composure, but he couldn't take his eyes off the alien, already imagining a photograph of him next to the tiny creature gracing the front page of every important newspaper in the country, being displayed behind the imposing talking head of every network newscaster.

The two walked closer and, before he had a chance to take a better look at the extraterrestrial creature, Harold Brainard grabbed one of Ben's arms, and the tiny entity latched on to his leg.

"What—?"

"Lead us," Harold said.

The alien's arms felt like long snakes wrapped around Ben's right knee.

Peering down at the small lavender man locked to him, Ben said, "My alien friend, I don't know much about you but I'm willing to learn. Let me tell you, you've hooked onto the right human. I'll make you famous, and you'll make me famous. We were made for each other."

"Lead us," repeated Harold.

Too disoriented and exhausted to argue the arrangement, Ben started back around the motel. Since the entity held tightly to his right leg, Ben had to swing it like it was a wooden prosthesis.

Harold had been clutching Ben's arm for mere seconds, but already the smell was returning.

"We have to help him get back in the air," Harold said.

As he swung his right leg, Ben looked down toward the tiny lavender man again and asked, "Why are you here, anyway?"

The words echoed through Ben's head. *I come. I go. That's what I do.*

He wouldn't ask anything else, not just now. Telepathic communication was something he didn't want to deal with at the moment. He'd already made enough reality adjustments for one day, thank you very goddamned much.

Here he was in Elderton, Illinois. He had the crashed UFO in his motel room and the alien itself clamped around his leg like a lovestruck dachshund.

No one could ever say that Ben Savitch didn't strive and suffer to get his story.

Of course, that wasn't the whole story. There was Almo Parrish and Chandler Quinn and Vida Proust and Frank Shepard. There was Audrey Gayle and Jeffrey Sprague.

If that weren't enough, another thought had intimated itself to Ben. If Chandler and Almo were dead, and there weren't any obits in the local paper at all, what kind of process had he given birth to? Would people begin dropping like flies, all the people who had died and never been told, leaving Elderton little more than a middling-sized burial ground? Would Ben Savitch's truth be more powerful than Elderton's innocent hope and ignorance?

"I don't even want to think about this," Ben said, opening the door to Room 23, bringing Harold Brainard and the alien inside with him. "Do you people hear me?" he said, sweeping his arm through the air. "I don't want to even think about all of this!"

"We hear you," Chandler said very quietly. "And, sadly enough, we believe you."

Ben noticed that there was an angry-looking blister on Chandler's left cheek.

Amazingly, not one person said a word about the fact that Ben had a lavender alien creature clinging to his body.

The entire room began to vibrate and rumble.

Ben said, "Oh, great. What now?"

Struggling to turn around with Harold and the lavender anthropoid attached to him, he nevertheless made it to the window and pulled aside the curtain.

The parking lot of the PrairieView Motel was rapidly filling.

A long queue of vans and motorhomes was pulling into the drive.

Most of them were white, and most of them had color-fully painted designs on the side, logos of the stations they represented.

A few of them had satellite dishes secured to their roofs.

It seemed everyone in the news business was arriving in Elderton. Moreover, each logo embodied a holy grail, a sacred goal, a dream that for too long had remained out of Ben Savitch's reach.

"My God," he heard himself say, "it's . . . an invasion."

"*The* invasion," Chandler said.

The motel room was swathed in silence. No one spoke, or even breathed.

"I'm on the deck of the Titanic," Ben finally muttered. "What do I want to do now?"

Part Three

The Opening Night

Chapter Thirty

Jeffrey sat on the very corner of the bed, sensing the faint cadence of Almo's breathing and the warmth of Miss Gayle's presence, feeling the quiet fear of Chandler Quinn and the confusion of the fuzzy-looking Frank Shepard and the unfocused grief of the blind man and the little lavender creature.

But when he looked at Ben Savitch, he didn't feel anything at all, and that worried him.

More and more, sitting in the motel room seemed every bit as confusing as sitting in the living rooms of the many foster homes in which he'd lived, where family members were hurting or confused and a lone adult remained incredibly oblivious to the drone of pain.

Here, Ben was the family member who wasn't responding to the drama that was unfolding with every second. The man didn't even seem nervous. He just looked around the room as he tapped a finger against his chin, as if he were doing nothing more important than thinking up an answer for a trivia game.

Didn't he see that Almo was dying? The Munchkin's face and neck and hands were covered with a forest of festering blisters. His skin was darkening and curling. His breathing was becoming shallower and less frequent, punctuated by faint shivers.

Come on, Mr. Savitch. Do something. Here, right now, you're the father. You can't ignore the pain. Do something.

As if he'd heard Jeffrey's thoughts, Ben raised an arm. "Okay, everyone quiet."

What's he talking about? Everybody is *quiet.*

"The first thing we're going to do is split up. We can't all just stay packed in here like this. I'll go see the night manager and get several more rooms."

"I don't need a room," Chandler said. His voice was now completely bereft of its contagious enthusiasm and fascination. He sounded tired, so tired. "I have my own home, and Frank here can give me a lift. True, he hasn't done too well at flying so far, but if he crash-lands and kills me, what's really been lost? At least I'll go out soaring."

Ben shook his head. "You can't just amble out into the parking lot and fly away. There are reporters swarming this place. We can't be reckless."

Chandler shrugged wearily. "Frank can move faster than a falling star—remember?—so that's not a concern. But I'd like Almo to come with us. We lived our lives together, both before and after. It seems fitting that we die together. My only hope is that I live long enough to figure out why he and I didn't die immediately upon learning the truth, whereas the Frehley boy did. We'll have to see if we can determine what became of Vida Proust, since that knowledge will apprise us of vital realities. What already is unambiguous is that the longer one remains dead before revivification, the more death seeks to manifest itself, as it did in Vida's case. Her parents were right: the town should have let her rest. It logically follows that the longer one labors under the delusion of aliveness, the longer it takes to . . . fade away. I'd bet, given time and the necessary data, I could reduce the process to a simple linear equation."

From the looks of it, Almo isn't all that far from fading away, Jeffrey thought.

"If you want to leave, I can't stop you," said Ben, waving a hand dismissively, as if he were wagging away a gnat.

"Benny Savitch!" Miss Gayle looked very unhappy. "Listen to yourself. I don't believe you. The least we owe Almo and Chandler is some company. They should stay. All of us should stay. I can take care of Almo—"

"Isn't Almo the same guy you thought was the center of Elderton's madness?" Ben said. He sounded impatient, like an angry foster parent, like he wanted everyone out of his sight. "And just how do you expect to help him anyway?"

Audrey lowered her head. "I can comfort him, at least."

Ben ignored her, now turning toward Harold Brainard, who stood holding hands with the little lavender man.

"You, Harold, I'll get a room for you to stay in."

Harold said, "What about my . . ." He tipped his head toward the entity.

"The alien stays here. No debate on that point. It remains with me."

Audrey stood and held out her hand to Jeffrey.

"I'm not going to stay around here while you divvy everyone up," she said. "Come, Jeffrey, let's go home."

It was bewildering the way Jeffrey's sentiments were shifting. He'd come back to town because he thought Ben Savitch might offer some security and guidance. Now, again, Miss Gayle seemed like the safest, most solid human being who had ever walked the earth. Maybe, in this one case, Jeffrey's first impression had been the best. He'd have to remember that.

"Tell you what," Chandler said, then paused a moment to cough. Faint wisps of foul-smelling smoke issued from his mouth with each hack. "Perhaps you can give Almo and Frank and me a ride," he croaked. Turning to the ragged image of Frank Shepard, he added, "No offense, my friend."

Frank looked concerned and disheartened, hands folded

in front of him as though he were at a funeral. "None taken," he buzzed.

"In fact," Audrey said. "Harold, you can come with us, too. There's no reason you should be stranded out here by yourself. You can stay at my house."

"Thank you," Harold said. "You can lead me."

Ben's eyes flared with anger. "Go ahead then, the whole damned bunch of you!"

Jeffrey couldn't understand. He'd thought Ben was the one person in this town who might have a little wisdom, but he seemed the most confused of everyone.

Ben stomped toward the door. "I don't need you! Hell, I came into this town innocently looking for a story. Sure, I'm sorry Almo's dying but, good lord, the guy actually bit the big one over twenty years ago. It's not like I killed him. Chandler killed him!"

Chandler frowned. "Now wait just one min—"

"No, *you* wait!" Ben continued, face taut and crimson. "The same thing with the Proust girl. Hell, all I did was tell the truth, pointing out something that was obvious to everyone in this town but nobody dared mention. And you're treating me like I'm some sort of murderer."

"I don't hear anyone treating you that way," Miss Gayle said, as gently and simply as if she were explaining an arithmetic problem to her students. "Maybe that's how you're feeling about yourself."

"Oh, Audrey, that's a buncha crap and you know it!"

She cringed. "Ben, Jeffrey's here. Try to speak like an adult."

Ben reached up to his temples like he might yank out some of his hair. "I've had it with all of you. I've had it with Elderton! I just want my story, all right?" He pointed to the little lavender man. "And I've got my story! At this point

188

you people are . . . distractions."

"Fair enough," Chandler said. "Perhaps he's right. Perhaps it's better this way."

Audrey said, "Yes, I think it is. Come on, everyone. Get ready. I'll go out and warm up the car. If I don't see any strangers outside, you can come out and we can get out of here."

She looked Ben in the eyes, and there seemed to be tears shining in hers. "You were nicer in first grade, Benny."

"Wasn't everyone?"

Someone pounded on the door.

"Shit!" Ben said. "Into the bathroom, all of you!"

"What about Almo?" asked Jeffrey.

Audrey sighed. "The rest of you, do what he says. I'll sit here with Almo."

She sat on the bed and gently stroked the head and cheeks of Almo Parrish, who had begun to shudder between his creaking breaths.

Chandler led the way, motioning Harold and Jeffrey and the blurring Frank and the little lavender man to follow him.

Once they were secured in the bathroom, Ben answered the door, opening it a crack.

"Ben, how the hell are you?"

"Hiya, Max."

"Surprised?"

"Yeah, you could say that."

"I don't know if you noticed, but not only did I bring a crew, but a few affiliates sent their people, too. Looks like you've got yourself one white-hot story here in Elderton."

"Yeah."

"What's the matter? I thought you'd spontaneously ejaculate when you saw me. I thought this was the best gift I could ever offer an old friend."

"Sorry. I'm just a little tired."

"Too tired to orient me to the story? You sure you're not sick or something?"

A weary laugh. "Believe it or not, I think I'm too tired. Tell you what, Max, how about if we both get ourselves some sleep tonight and tomorrow I'll let you in on everything. I'll try to put it together in my head tonight and lay it all out for you tomorrow. It'll be worth the wait, believe me. You've never seen or heard anything like I'm going to be sharing with you. Never."

"I guess. If that's the way you want it, Ben. Call me in the morning. I'll treat you to breakfast if there's anywhere decent to eat in this godforsaken place."

"Yeah," Ben said. "That sounds good."

He closed the door.

"Are you going to tell him everything?" Audrey asked.

Ben's voice was flat. "I'm a journalist. That's my job. Until I saw the news crews driving in here, I'd almost forgotten that. But yeah. It's my job."

She shook her head and almost looked like she pitied him. "I guess you're right."

"I don't like your tone, Audrey."

"Benny, I don't really care."

He made a sound, a grunt or snort. "And you? You came here to build a nest. Do you call driving away from me with a carful of misfits building a nest?"

She smiled. "Yes, I do."

Chapter Thirty-One

Frank Shepard couldn't stop looking at his hands.

They looked like they were evaporating, dissolving into the air. The fingertips weren't rounded or smooth anymore; his neatly manicured nails were barely visible; he was slowly smearing into nothingness.

Frank sat in the back seat of Audrey's car between Almo and Chandler. Almo was unconscious, leaning against the door, breaths coming further and further apart.

At least Frank had done one thing right, carrying Almo to the car without dropping and killing him. But other than that, what had he done? What service had he fulfilled for humanity? Frank Shepard—Sky-Lord—hadn't performed one constructive, heroic act and people were dying on either side of him, the people who seemed to matter the most in this existence to which he had been abruptly awakened.

Life, it seemed, was sapping his strength and will, driving him to his knees.

He turned to Chandler, holding his hands out in front of him. "Look at what's happening to me," he said. His voice sounded crackly, like an ancient, poorly tuned radio.

Chandler gently patted him on the back and Frank was grateful that, even as he was withering into nonexistence, he could feel Chandler's tender touches of encouragement and care.

"I know, my friend, and I apologize," Chandler said. "I had no right to force you into being. Does it hurt, the fading?"

"No, it doesn't."

"For that I'm thankful. You don't deserve to hurt, Frank."

"Neither do you, Mr. Quinn."

Chandler's burst of laughter quickly transformed into a series of racking coughs. "You might . . . find some disagreement on that point, I'm afraid."

"What can I do? I want to help, but my mind's becoming cloudy and thick. I can't think of what I can do to help . . . anyone. And that's what I'm for. That's the *only* thing I'm for."

"I wish I could proffer something useful, my friend. I don't know what any of us can do except to sit and wait for our individual fadings to run their course. We are dwindling together, my superhuman ally."

Jeffrey poked his head over the front seat. "Why can't he just throw everyone out of Elderton except those of us who belong here? He's Sky-Lord!"

After another assault of coughs, Chandler croaked, "Too late for that, my youthful cogitator. The surf is swelling and rolling, and there's nothing left for us to do except ride the wave."

"We're not riding the wave," Jeffrey said. "We're drowning."

After letting off the three men at Chandler's house—Frank carrying the unconscious Almo over one shoulder—Audrey silently drove Jeffrey and Harold to her home. She seemed wearier with each step she took up the driveway, so much so that, to Jeffrey's eyes, it looked as though she were mimicking Vida Proust.

As she fumbled in her purse for the house keys, Jeffrey said, "Is there anything I can do to help, Miss Gayle?"

She unlocked and opened the door. "Nothing I can think of, Jeffrey."

"How about me?" Harold asked, also sounding drained. "What should I do now? I'm lost again, I think."

"I don't know what to tell you, Harold. I'm sorry."

"Then I'll walk." He turned from them and without uttering another word, shuffled down the driveway, took a knowing left on the sidewalk, and disappeared into the darkness.

"Good night, Harold," said Jeffrey.

Too late. Harold was gone.

Once in the house, Audrey plodded to her bedroom and closed the door.

A few minutes later, standing in the hallway, Jeffrey thought he heard her crying.

He washed his face. Then, exhausted, he trudged to the bedroom—the one he would have shared with Bert Frehley—and lay down.

As dead tired as his body was, his mind wouldn't shut off, wouldn't even slow down. It was as though a thousand voices were simultaneously discussing and lecturing and arguing and talking absurdly fast, too fast for him to follow.

Perhaps by now, having had the experiences in all the foster homes, all the times he'd been given up on and moved, he should have known better than to expect adults to solve problems. And that didn't make sense. Didn't they have the wisdom and the years of living to tell them that there was *always* something they could do? As years passed, did life take such a toll that by the time someone was middle-aged, they saw only thunderheads of problems and never the sunbeams of solutions? Everyone was giving up. Even Miss Gayle, it seemed.

As he lay there thinking, two things his Mom used to tell him suddenly appeared in his mind as if they were being projected in fluorescent letters on a movie screen. They were stand-alone statements, no longer having any referents or situations to which they could be attached.

"Jeffrey, you can't do everything at once, but you *can* do *something* at once."

"The most precious things you can do for other people are the things they never find out about."

He opened the bedside table's drawer and pulled out a tablet of writing paper and a pen.

"Of course," he said aloud. "Why didn't anyone else think of this?"

And then he wrote in a gleeful fever, page after page, until he succumbed to deep, dreamless sleep, the pen still gripped in his hand.

Chapter Thirty-Two

"Just take a drink, would you?" Ben said, kneeling in front of the lavender entity, who sat on the floor, leaning against the wall.

What is this?

"It's called Mountain Dew. I would say something about it tickling your innards, but I'm not sure if you have any innards to tickle."

Gripping it with both hands, the entity held the green can close to its tiny mouth then turned away its head.

I cannot.

"How about some cheese curls then?" He ripped open the tiny bag he'd purchased from the vending machine in the motel office and tipped it toward the entity. "They're nutritious."

No.

Exasperated, fresh out of ideas, Ben flung the bag across the room, a handful of the garish orange morsels pinwheeling out and scattering across the threadbare motel carpeting.

"You've got to eat something," Ben said. Then he added, "Don't you?"

I don't know.

"Well, hell, if you don't know, who does?"

I don't know.

"For Christ's sake. You look like you're sick or something. You need to stay well for a day or two. You're the capper of my story. You're going to be a national phenomenon."

I don't know.

Ben rummaged through his overnight bag until he unearthed his 35mm camera.

"Mind if I get a few shots? Just to get you accustomed to the flash and everything?"

I don't know.

"I'll take that as a yes." He pried off the lens cap and attached the flash unit.

"Are you ready? Let me guess—"

I don't know.

"Say 'cheese curls!' "

Ben snapped four photographs of the lavender entity sitting bent and weary on the floor.

"Great! Now let's put you next to your spacecraft."

The entity didn't move of its own accord, so Ben picked it up by one arm and carried it over next to the teardrop-shaped UFO, which sat throbbing in the corner.

The entity didn't seem to want to stand up, so finally Ben let it lean against the craft. It wasn't a dynamic pose, but it would have to do for now.

He took three more pictures.

"Great," Ben said, replacing the lens cap and returning the camera to his overnight bag. "I'll tell you what. As excited as I am, I'm going to have to try and get a little shut-eye so I can be fresh for tomorrow. Do you sleep, at least?"

I don't know. I come. I go. That is what I do.

"Where do you want to rest? I mean, there's only room for one in the bed, you know. Nothing personal."

The entity struggled to turn, almost falling in the process. Then, still leaning against its craft, it traced its lithe, tiny fingers around the rip in the side of the ship before lifting itself up and slowly crawling inside.

It sat in its seat, crossed its arms over its small chest, then quit moving.

"Okay, now if you need anything, you wake me up, okay? You need to stay well. Understand?"

Ben turned off the overhead light, crawled into bed, set his alarm for five-thirty, and clicked off the table lamp.

As he lay there in the darkness—glimmering with the excitement of his impending fame—he couldn't help but think of Audrey. He couldn't remember a time when he had met a woman who had so thoroughly charmed and enticed him without even trying. He felt something for her, something deep and warm, a connection like he'd never imagined, much less experienced.

Too bad. There were other, more consequential things to consider. He was a professional, after all, and he regarded his profession as seriously as a neurosurgeon regarded skull carpentry. This was the story of his career—once in a lifetime—and to turn away from it would be the eternal capstone of the series of failures that defined Ben's adult life.

He had been driving down that infinite straightaway too long, left blinker blinking. This might be his last opportunity to make a turn and travel down a road that offered something more than endless vistas of defeat and frustration.

Maybe she'd understand. Maybe after his story ran and he'd been hired away by some gigantic news organization, she would see the wisdom of his decision. And if she didn't . . . well, perhaps she wasn't the type of woman who could ever be a true partner to him anyway. Yes, of course. This wasn't a test of Ben, really. This was a test of Audrey.

He turned over and faced the pulsing spacecraft. Even in the dark, he could make out its mute, moist glow.

I wonder if this little booger's going to stay alive long enough for me to present him to the world, Ben thought.

I don't know, the entity thought back.

Chapter Thirty-Three

For the first time in his life, dawn didn't break too early for Ben Savitch.

In fact, by the time the sun barely nuzzled the flush Midwestern horizon, Ben had showered, shaved, dressed in reasonably fashionable clothing, and gathered the notes he'd scribbled after awakening in the middle of the night.

Each story had its own rhythm. Each story needed to unfold by its own distinct design to effect maximum dramatic impact. In his notes he had crafted nothing less than the perfect progression of revelations that he would present to Max: the Presence Chamber, Harold Brainard, Vida Proust (if she could be found), Chandler and Almo (if they were still breathing), Frank Shepard (if he were still visible). Then and only then would Ben reveal the alien and its spacecraft.

Perfect. Compelling. Irresistible.

He peeked through the breach in the spacecraft's hull. The entity opened its tiny eyes and turned its head his way.

"Good morning, my tiny ticket to Somewhereville," Ben said, trying his best to put on a newsman smile. It never hurt to practice.

The alien didn't respond, not even with a vague telepathic aside.

"I'm happy you're alive. I mean that," Ben said. "Hell, I'm happy *I'm* alive and it's not often you'd hear me spew those words."

I need to go.

"To the bathroom? Well, I'll tell you, I don't really see

how—considering you don't seem to have any of the necessary fleshy apparatuses—but if you need to relieve yourself—"

*I need to go. Away from here. Up. Away. I come. I go. That
is what I do.*

"Let me tell you, partner, there's a lot to be said for not
going home again. Take it from an expert. It's not what you
remember, if you're more intact than me and you can remember it at all. What star system are you from, anyway?
Ganymede? Andromeda? Sirius? Hurry up, tell me. I don't
know many more."

I don't know. I come. I go.

"Yeah, right. So that means you're—"

Nobody. Don't you recognize me?

"Bottom line: whoever or whatever the hell you are, at
least you're alive. I'm going to be gone for awhile and I
promise you I'll try to find some way for you to get away
from here. Back up in the sky, among the stars, all of that."

Thank you.

Not only did Ben hang the Do Not Disturb sign on the
outside knob as he left, he also made a brief stop at the
motel office, where Sophie Ardell still sat as noble sentry.
She agreed that, because all of Ben's momentous professional work was in Room 23, she'd inform Housekeeping
not to enter, although she emphasized that if he needed
anything, anything at all, he shouldn't hesitate even a
second to let her know.

At Ben's request, Sophie looked up Max's room
number. Within seconds, Ben was hammering the door of
Room 42.

Max looked to have gotten up as early as Ben. Perhaps it
was from all his experience, but he looked so sparkish and
natty that he could have sat down behind a fancy desk and

delivered the network news that instant. He was so perfectly put together even his eyebrows appeared deftly combed.

Ben and Max drove to Duane and Joyce's for a couple of cups of coffee and some heavenly cream-filled pastries.

Several times, locals ambled up smiling, shaking Ben's hand.

"Nice to have you back, son."

"We're proud of you, Benny."

"We've missed you and your folks. Welcome home."

Didn't these people know that Ben was single-handedly unraveling Elderton's strangeness, that Vida and Almo and Chandler were all fading into the void because of him? Talk about forgiveness.

Max said, "You're quite the celebrity, it seems. What a guy."

"Yeah."

Chuckling to himself, Max began pressing in earnest for Ben to reveal his secrets. "C'mon, now. Don't tell me that being in this catatonic ward of a town has rendered you mentally sluggish, too, Ben. Out with it."

"A little at a time, Maxipad," Ben said, waving away Maggie the waitress, who had come to see if they wanted a fresh cup.

"Okay, what's first then, Ben? Let's get started while the day is young."

"I'll show you a place where Elderton takes their children . . . blindfolded."

The combed eyebrows levitated. "You're kidding. Not like that thing Sallee reported on up in Chicago?"

"No, nothing like that, but strange just the same. And remember, Max, this is only the beginning, the opening chapter of an ever-expanding saga. You can start thinking full-length documentary, buddy."

"If blindfolded kids are the beginning, then what's the ending?"

"Wouldn't you like to know? I'd hate to tell you and broil your frontal lobes so early in the morning."

Max curled his nose like the senior judge at a flatulence contest. "This is your big story? Bagfuls of old cloth that they make the children sniff? I mean, come on, Ben, you've got to be kidding. This is your legendary story?"

Ben chuckled with shrugging confidence, a dollop of smugness thrown in for good measure. "Just laying a little groundwork, Padster. Doesn't this strike you as just the tee-niest bit psychotic, having kids smell patches of old clothing so they can reconnect to the past? And the effect does seem to be powerful. You should have seen the reaction a woman I know had when she smelled her father—"

"Might make a good little human interest piece—two minutes at the end of a boring broadcast—but no, it's nothing special, nothing I'd get Wally the cameraman out of bed to shoot. Take a close look, Ben. We're talkin' rag bags here."

Ben slammed the filing cabinet closed. "Okay, then. What will it take to pique your professional curiosity?"

"Take a wild guess, Ben. An alien, buddy. An honest-to-goodness straight-from-outer-space bug-eyed no-eared alien."

"Hmm," Ben said, looking at the floor as he mentally dismantled the tidy progression of revelations he'd planned. He couldn't lose Max's interest. Success was too close. "Okay. I can do that."

Ben threw open the door to his motel room, swept his hand in a grand semi-circle and said, "Ta-da!"

Max followed him into the room, eyes riveted on the

pulsing UFO crammed into the corner.

"This is it, huh? You have a UFO in your room," Max said. "Doesn't the management have rules against this?"

"Get closer, Max. Feel it. Then—if you dare—look inside."

Wiping one hand back over his silver wavy hair, Max crept closer.

He touched the side of the craft. "It feels kind of gooey."

"Yeah, you betcha," Ben said, sounding like a car salesman busting proud over a new model. "I don't know what's it's made of, but it's not earthly."

Max nodded, but none too enthusiastically. "You think so? I've seen B-movie special effects more convincing than this."

Ben was undeterred. "Peek inside, Pad de la Max."

Max peered through the tattered hole in the side of the craft. "A lavender guy, huh? I thought they were gray with potato heads and wide black eyes."

"Those are the rumors, Max. This is reality. Or at least one of them."

"I see."

Ben was getting concerned. "You don't seem nearly as excited as I thought you'd be."

"The thing isn't moving," Max said.

Frowning, Ben pushed Max aside, reached into the craft, grabbed the alien by the arm and pulled it through the hole.

It flopped in his grasp like a puppet, even though its eyes were wide open.

"It gets like this sometimes, I don't know why. Hell, I even tried to feed it some cheese curls last night, just in case it was hungry. It wouldn't eat."

"Cheese curls. Interesting choice."

I need to go. Up. I come. I go. That is what I do.

"There," Ben said, pointing at the alien. "Did you hear that? It communicates telepathically."

Max paused briefly, then shook his head, looking into Ben's eyes with something akin to clinical concern. "No, I didn't hear anything. You're hearing an alien voice in your head?"

Ben shrugged. "Well . . . yeah."

"Okay," Max said. "Well, it looks like you have quite a story here."

"Your words say one thing. Your tone says another."

"It's just this, Ben: if we parade out this display in front of the other affiliates, much less try to sell it to the networks, they're going to laugh their asses off and say it's phony. You saw the alien autopsy deal on Fox. I mean, a Special Effects intern at a community college could put together something that looked more authentic than this. You know, as much as I had to cajole the others to come, they're not going to stay here too long. Downstate Illinois isn't exactly a Mecca for luxurious R and R, you know. We need to see something, Ben. We need to see something by tonight."

"Jesus Christ, Max, I just showed you an extraterrestrial spacecraft and a goddamned alien, and you're saying it's not enough?" Sheesh, and Ben thought *he* was a hardened reporter.

"Not these days, my friend. Not any more. Appearances are everything, and this looks like a Hasbro playset for rich kids."

"What do you need then? Want me to get a doctor down here to examine the creature and tell you it's an authentic alien? Or see if I can find a sheriff to attest to the crash? What do you need? These things are real, Padling. Arrange for your own experts to come down here, anybody you choose, I don't give a damn. The craft and the alien will pass any test you could design. C'mon, I dare you."

Max clasped his hands behind his back and looked at the ceiling. "No time for all those silly arrangements, and to do it right would be awfully expensive, especially if this all ends up being as fake as it looks. We don't have time to dilly-dally here in Nowhere, Illinois. We need to see the damned thing fly, with the alien inside. Yeah, you arrange that and we'll have—more importantly—*you'll* have the story of the century."

"I can understand that, but the craft's damaged."

"No one around that can fix this type of vehicle, eh? No alien body shops in this mystic village?"

Ben suddenly broke into laughter. Clapping his hands together, he said, "Hell, yes, there *is* someone who can fix it. Crazy inventor named Chandler Quinn. He even built a machine and was able to reanimate . . . well, I'll save that story for another time."

"He can fix it? By tonight?"

"If he's still alive." Ben pictured the blisters that had begun appearing on Chandler the last time he saw him, the puffs of old smoke issuing from his mouth. Of course, there was no guaranteeing that Chandler—or anyone in Elderton for that matter—had much interest in helping the man who had come to town, run over a dog and proceeded to dismantle their psychotic sorcery. And yet . . . most everyone in town had treated Ben with almost giddy deference.

Hell yes, it was worth a try.

"What does that mean, 'if he's still alive?' " Max asked.

"Long story. But let's say that at dusk tonight, you and every damned camera you can drag there will get footage of a UFO and its occupant taking off and flying to the stars.

Close-ups and everything. Right behind the PrairieView Motel."

"I'd say there are awards in it for you, if not for all of us, not to mention a unique place in history."

"Then that's what's going to happen."

Chapter Thirty-Four

"Jeffrey, it's Saturday morning. What are you doing up so early? It's not even seven-thirty."

Jeffrey stood next to Audrey's bed, his body quaking with excitement. Under his arm he clutched several sheets of scribbled-on notebook paper.

"I want you to take me to Mr. Quinn's house," he said, adjusting his Chicago Cubs cap.

"For heaven's sake, why?"

"I want to help Almo and Mr. Quinn. I think I know how." He handed her the papers. "Almo's sicker, so I think I should talk to him first."

Sitting up in bed, she unfolded the stack of papers and read quickly.

Smiling, she tousled Jeffrey's hair. "You know something? Not only are you a bright boy, but you've also got the best and biggest heart of anyone I've ever met."

Scuffing the floor with the toe of his shoe, Jeffrey blushed.

"I understand what you're thinking, Jeffrey. Mind if I make some minor corrections, just so it reads better? A little editing?"

"Nope. I was hoping you'd say that."

"Go pour yourself some cereal. When you're done eating, we'll take a trip over to Chandler's house. But I want to warn you: just don't get your hopes—" She stopped herself in midsentence.

"Don't what?"

Smiling, she said, "Never mind."

Upon arriving at Chandler's house, they found a wilting Chandler and a blurry Frank Shepard huddled next to the bed where Almo slept fitfully, if indeed it could have been called sleep. At times his body would jerk—an arm here, a leg there—and then he would settle back into his frozen slumber.

Chandler got up and when he did, his body bent like he'd aged a hundred years since the night before. A fierce pattern of blisters covered his face. He shuffled to Jeffrey and Audrey, and whispered in a weak, hoarse voice, "Bless your hearts for coming to pay your respects. I don't know how much longer our dear friend will be with us on this planet."

Audrey said, "Actually, this was Jeffrey's idea. He wrote something that he wants to read to Almo."

Chandler's blistered face creased into a smile. "A written tribute? You're a good boy, Jeffrey. You're going to be a good man someday. I wish I were going to be around to witness your ripening."

"Thanks, Mr. Quinn. Can I, uh, can I be alone with Almo for a little while? A few minutes?"

"Why of course, my young good-hearted icon." He turned and motioned for Audrey and the blinking Frank Shepard to follow him out of the room.

Jeffrey closed the creaking door until it latched, then sat down in the chair next to Almo's bed. His opened his papers and cleared his throat. "Almo? Mr. Parrish? I want you to listen to me if you're in there somewhere, okay? I've got something I need to read to you."

Almo turned his head to one side but didn't open his eyes or show any sign of consciousness.

Jeffrey cleared his throat again. "Okay. You see, the

problem is that you didn't find the next day's paper back in Mr. Savitch's room, the one after the day of the car accident. I looked it up and listen to what I found. Are you listening? It's all right here: '*The Journal-Star* regrets that an error was made in yesterday's story regarding the auto accident involving Almo Parrish and Chandler Quinn of Elderton, Illinois. As it turns out, our reporter received erroneous information and, besides suffering amnesia and minor scrapes and burns, the two men are now resting comfortably—' "

A little swollen hand touched Jeffrey's arm.

Jeffrey looked up.

One of Almo's eyes was open and the last Munchkin had a faint smile drawn across his darkened, peeling face.

Tears flowed from Jeffrey's eyes. "Mr. Parrish! It worked!"

Almo's voice was as faint as the autumn breeze outside. "You're such a good boy, Jeffrey."

"You're feeling better then? You're going to be all right?"

Almo pulled in a deep, wheezing breath. "Yes, I'm going to be all right. But, no, I'm not going to live."

"Why not? I thought—"

"I know what you thought, my boy, and it's the most wonderful, magical, loving thing anyone's ever done for me. But you see, I've been dying a little while now, and I think I want to keep going. It's a road I haven't traveled before and, from what I've seen so far, it's magic, too. Exciting. Yellow bricks and everything."

"Why would you want to die?"

"I've had more than my share of life. Think of it: I was given the gift to predict the first falling leaf every autumn; I was privileged to sense the condition of the town and its citizens every moment and even knew that we were going to be invaded; I got to be looked up to all these years . . . even though I'm a small man."

"You're the biggest man I ever met."

"In the forest of people, Jeffrey, I've been able to be a mighty oak, for a little while at least. It's more than I could ever have dreamed of, all those years when I was mowing lawns and scooping snow. But you know something? *Those* years were magic, too. It's all been magic. It all *is* magic. All along."

"You can't die," Jeffrey said, holding tightly to Almo's shuddering arm. "You're everything to this town. All the good magic will be gone."

Almo closed his eyes and shook his head. "No, it won't. You're every bit as magical as I am. And I'm . . . tired. While I don't recommend it to you for a long, long time, for me this dying feels rather good. It's like Chandler once said: death is the period at the end of the sentence of life. Just like a sentence needs a period for it to make sense, so does life need an end for it to have meaning. I think . . . I think it's time for the period to be written at the end of my sentence. And really, Jeffrey, believe me, I don't mind. No regrets."

"But if I'm magic, how come I couldn't bring you back to life?"

"I'm talking to you, aren't I?" Almo said, eyes still closed.

"Yeah, but—"

"I'll tell you what, Jeffrey. Let me give you a little hint. I've known my friend Chandler for many years. His mind is so open that it wants to reach out and pull the universe to its chest and hug it as tightly as it can. Something tells me he hasn't yet reached the period at the end of his sentence. Why don't you take Chandler into the kitchen and read him the same story you just read to me? I can almost guarantee that you'll witness something miraculous."

"Really?"

Almo didn't respond. His body had sunk back down into the bed, and that moment he looked smaller than a Munchkin.

Jeffrey stood up, bent over, and kissed the last Munchkin on his blistered forehead. He wiped his eyes as he walked out of the bedroom.

"Are you all right, my youthful compatriot?" Chandler said. He was sitting on the couch between Miss Gayle and Frank Shepard, whose image rippled, fading in and out of focus like it was underwater.

"I'm fine," Jeffrey answered, trying to smile.

"Did you read the article you found to Mr. Parrish?" asked Audrey.

"Yes, I did. And he opened his eyes and listened to me and talked to me for a minute."

Chandler leapt to his feet, then quickly bent over and pressed one hand against his back as pain racked him. "You're serious?" he asked, wincing. "He was awake? What did he say?"

"He said I should take you into the kitchen and read this to you."

"If that's what my tiny confidant proposed, then that's precisely what we'll do. Come, Jeffrey, lead the way. I'm anxious to hear what magic you'll share with me."

Chapter Thirty-Five

Startled when Audrey opened Chandler's front door, at first Ben didn't know how to react. He scrutinized her face for any traces of hatred or murderous intent and, thankfully, found none. Painfully cool indifference, though: that was there somewhere.

She looked him square in the eyes for several moments before saying, "What do you want here?"

"Well, to be honest, I'd like to talk to Chandler."

"Chandler, as you know better than anyone, is not feeling too well."

He felt like an unwelcome vacuum cleaner salesman, like there wasn't any relationship between Audrey and him at all and what she wanted more than anything was for their interaction to die a quick death and for him to fade away quicker than Frank the flagging Sky-Lord.

"Still," Ben said, trying to remain as gentle and courteous as possible, "if I could just see him for a minute."

She opened the door. As Ben passed her, she said, "You know something, Benny? You were the nicest kid in first grade, full of life and laughter, everything that matters. Elderton gave you those gifts, more than you'll ever know. I wonder how you managed to lose them all. I wonder if you'll find them again."

How does one respond to that? It was kind of like the old question about how badly you thrash your wife. No escape. "Beats me," he answered. "Life, I guess. Maybe life stole them from me."

"Life's not a thief, Benny," Audrey said. "When you and

211

your family left Elderton, you took those gifts with you. You didn't lose them. Somehow, somewhere, you threw them away."

She turned on her heel. "I'll see if Chandler's up to a visitor . . . particularly you."

Ben felt smaller than Almo, like he was so small he could easily be stomped beneath Audrey's heel and end up a flattened gob of offal on the sole of her shoe. Obviously whatever bridge he'd begun to build with her had been felled in a major demolition project. Something told him he'd been the foreman of that particular undertaking.

His dim sense of regret was supplanted by shock when Chandler came bounding into the living room, laughing and looking even younger and healthier than when Ben first met him. Not only was his face free of blisters and sores but his skin was rosy, and he carried himself with the dynamic ease of a teenager.

"Ben Savitch," he said, bowing formally, "what can I do for you this banner day on planet Earth?"

He extended his hand. Ben grabbed it and Chandler squeezed and pumped so energetically that Ben thought he might be driven to his knees.

"Chandler . . . you're looking . . . great."

"And why shouldn't I? Ben, my friend, the boundless power of the human mind is staggering. Think of it: my hearing an erroneous narrative of my own demise led to a psychosomatic manifestation of the injuries I imagined I'd sustained. Thank goodness Jeffrey Sprague found the correction to the article that your August newspaper issued the following day. If I hadn't been set straight, I would likely be at death's door instead of standing here talking to you, feeling as fit as the proverbial Stradivarius."

"Jeffrey found out that the story was a mistake?" Ben

frowned. Errors like that weren't made.

"The details regarding Almo's and my mortal fates, at least. That's right. Unfortunately, Almo wasn't as lucky as I. He apparently is so far gone even hearing the truth won't revive him now. But he seems to have made his peace with death. For that, I'm so thankful. Almo's an admirable human specimen, isn't he?"

Ben noticed Audrey standing behind Chandler's back. The pinched expression on her face—coupled with the wide, almost bugging eyes—instructed him to keep his mouth shut about any suspicions. He decided to do just that. He was a slow learner at times, but he *was* a learner.

"I'm happy Jeffrey found that out for you," Ben said. "As it turns out, it works out perfectly all the way around. Can I bend your ear for a moment?"

"Son, not only can you bend my ear, you can fold it over and secure it to my skull with a ten-penny nail."

"I came over to ask you if you think you can repair the alien craft."

Chandler laughed heartily. "Ben Savitch, at this very moment I think I could raise the Titanic barehanded. I have no doubts about my restorative abilities, not a one."

Audrey said, "Why would you want to do that now?"

"So the alien can take off tonight and return to wherever it came from," Ben answered. "It seems to be getting weak or ill, maybe even dying. It wants to leave. Chandler was the only person I could think of who could possibly fix the spacecraft."

"You have an exceptional level of ratiocination, my jour-nalistic crony," said Chandler. "Let me assemble some tools. Will you give me a ride? I'm not sure the Rambler is functional this morning."

"Sure."

After Chandler vaulted away to collect his tools, Audrey again walked close to Ben.

"What's in it for you, Benny?"

"What do you mean?"

"I mean that I've learned a lot about you the past day. I know you wouldn't just help an alien out of a sense of compassion or concern, and certainly not out of a sense of obligation. You wouldn't do it unless there was something in it for you."

"Honestly?"

"Of course . . . if you're able."

Ben sighed and looked at the floor. "All the news organizations will only stay through tonight. If they don't see the UFO take off with the alien inside, there won't be a story."

"That I can believe. Still thinking of Ben Savitch and only Ben Savitch."

It wasn't like she didn't have a point, but Ben felt her words burrowing beneath his skin and biting a little too much. "Listen, Audrey, for a kind, understanding, educated lady, you can be judgmental as hell when it comes to me. I'm talking about an important story here, the biggest story of my career. I'm a journalist, Audrey. That's what I am."

"No, Ben. You don't get it, do you?" She poked her finger against his chest. "*This* is what you are. You know what your trouble is, Ben?"

He sighed. "What?"

"You dream big," Audrey said, "but you live small."

A crash issued from the next room.

Practicing his flying, the frayed-around-the-edges Frank Shepard had streaked right into a large framed painting of a sleeping dog that hung in Chandler's dining room.

Chandler burst into the room and knelt next to Frank,

brushing shards of broken glass off the flickering image. Then he turned his eyes toward Ben and Audrey. "I sure wish I could repair *him*."

"Tell me how to help, how to matter," Frank said, "before I'm gone."

Chapter Thirty-Six

The old abandoned well had been cold, so cold. Cold and deep and hard and dark. But mostly cold.

Vida Proust stood on the square, gazing at the statue of lustrous white marble standing atop the red courthouse dome. It was a blindfolded woman facing south, holding scales in one hand, a large book in the other: justice and faith, the two things that Vida could neither feel nor dream of that moment. She'd hoped that by studying the statue, the blindfolded lady might tell her the things she needed to know. But the lady stood silently, not even noticing the little girl was looking up at her.

As she brought down her head and tried to look around, the muscles of her neck—cold as the well, hard as its bricks—resisted every millimeter of movement. It didn't hurt to move, but the way her body was freezing and turning solid as stone was itself a harrowing breed of pain. It would have felt almost good to ache, to hurt. This instant, Vida mourned those lost parts of life.

As she mourned, she also yearned for light and warmth and faith and wonder. She prayed to see bright colors again and to feel the dance of the wind against her skin and the sensation of blood washing through her body.

But she couldn't. All she could feel was the coldness and hardness and darkness of the well.

"Are you lost?" a voice said.

It was much too difficult to force words from her mouth, so she simply yanked one heavy leg from the ground, jerked it to one side, and set it down again. If she were lucky, she would be able to turn far enough to see who was talking to her.

Harold Brainard stood there, appearing as a tall mountain of a man. He bent his knees, lowering himself until he was eye-level with her.

He reached out and touched her shoulder, apparently unafraid to feel the way she was dying. The last time she had seen her mother and father, they were unable to touch her, consumed by grief without climax, mourning without loss. They loved her so much, she knew, but even parents had limits beyond which they could not travel.

"You've been left behind, haven't you?" Harold said, letting his hand lightly stroke her back, up and down. If she concentrated, she could almost feel it.

She tried to nod, but her head moved only a half-inch upward, paused, then moved a half-inch downward. She knew he couldn't see, but it was the best she could do.

"I know you're feeling bad and you're hurting and scared. I want to hold you for a while. Can I do that?"

With ardent care, Harold lifted her up and draped Vida over his left shoulder, as if she were a freshly-fed baby ready for burping.

She liked it. It brought back memories nearly vivid enough to push away the well. Facing the ground, she focused upon the passing lengths of sidewalk, noticing every jagged crack and every blade of dying grass poking through in a play for sunlight.

Harold walked slowly around the square, occasionally greeting those who passed them.

She heard a few of them say, "Hello, Vida. We love you, you know," or "You're the best little girl, Vida Proust." How nice it was for Mr. Brainard to carry her, to let her hear these things.

She closed her eyes, relaxing with the gentle rocking of Harold's steps.

"What would you like?" Harold asked.

Vida concentrated for a long long time. When she opened her mouth, her jaw muscles locked up, fought her.

Finally she was able to say: "Tell . . . me . . . a . . . story."

"I will," said Harold. "In fact, I'd love to. And if you want to go to sleep while I'm talking, please don't feel badly. You deserve to rest. You deserve anything you want."

She felt herself smile a little, which surprised her. She wished Harold could see her face.

"I feel like I just woke up, Vida," Harold said. "I feel like the clouds have burned away and I'm filled with radiant sunlight."

She'd never heard Harold Brainard talk this way. She liked it.

"It was long before you were born, but there was a time I could see. It was nice seeing, though it hasn't been bad being blind either. Until recently, I didn't know why I became blind, but I found out. You see, I saw something terrible happen, people I cared for dying and somehow . . . somehow . . . I think I saved them. It's like I had been storing all the magic that I'd collected growing up in Elderton and something told me that moment was the time and place I should use it. So I did. And you know something? It worked. That makes me very happy and proud.

"But I'm not sure. It seems like before I used everything I'd stored, the magic in Elderton was quiet and reverent, not the least bit showy or dramatic. Hope came to all of us as a matter of course. When I saved my friends, my hope was loud. Since then, I think the magic in Elderton has become loud, too, and more dramatic. I saved my friends, but

I'm not sure what I did to Elderton.

"Anyway, now there's no reason for me to be blind anymore. The magic I shared that day withdrew when the men found out the truth about what happened to them. There wasn't any reason for me to forget anymore, to keep the secret I'd promised myself I'd keep forever. The memories of that magical moment returned to me. So I've been walking around wondering why I still can't see, and I think I've finally figured it out.

"The magic I received from Elderton, it's still inside me, floating around somewhere. I didn't really use it at all. And maybe I could use it to bring back my sight, but for me to be the best Harold Brainard I can be, I think I need to find a way to reclaim my vision by giving magic to someone not expecting it, or perhaps someone not even deserving it. To just let it go. Keeping it forever by letting loose of it. Does that make sense? It sure did when I was thinking it.

"When I felt you standing there, I wondered if there were some way I could bring you magic without your expecting it. But I can't think of how. I know the things you want, I could feel them. You want light and warmth and faith and wonder, don't you?

"Perhaps if I keep walking, something will come to me.

"Are you feeling all right, Vida? Is this comfortable?"

Vida didn't respond, having drifted into restful sleep.

Chapter Thirty-Seven

Between the rear of the PrairieView Motel and the large field whose countless rows of dying corn extended to the edge of the visible earth, a collection of at least thirty people—reporters, camera operators, producers, sound crews—sat in lawn chairs drinking beers, talking, and laughing. A few of them had already set up their cameras, facing north. Three vans sat alongside the group, the satellite dishes on their roofs already having been locked into transmission position.

Inside Room 23 of the PrairieView Motel, Chandler turned to the rippling visage of Frank Shepard and said, "Frank, would you hand me—oh, let's see—how about that roll of duct tape?"

Chandler's sleeves were rolled up to the elbows and a thin sheen of perspiration shimmered on his forehead.

The entity lay on the bed, Ben sitting next to it. "You think you're close to being finished, Chandler?" he asked, his attentive gaze never straying from the lavender being.

"Not only do I think I'm close to finished, I would venture to guess that this craft will be airworthy within forty-five seconds . . . or fifty-four, if we continue to converse."

"Sorry." Ben reached down and patted the entity's arm. "Are you feeling better?"

I need to go. Time to fly. I come. I go. I must go now. It does not matter where. I am never lost. I must go. Up. That is what I do.

"That's exactly what's going to happen, little man. Just a few more hours and you'll be on your way." He stood, then

220

leaned down near the entity's face. "In fact, in just a few more hours, we're both going to be on our way."

To Chandler, Ben said, "I think I'll go outside and let everyone know that take-off is a definite go."

"Do what you need to," Chandler said, carefully applying a line of duct tape to the side of the craft, and pressing it down with such precision he might have been completing delicate surgery. "We'll do what we need to do in here."

"That's just it," Frank said, voice crackling and fizzing. "I don't know what *I* need to do." Now, even the image of his head was twinkling, bending left and right like a candle's flame in a breeze.

"In the majestic blueprint of life, I don't know either, my paling partner, but for at this moment, what you can do is hand me that small container of Vaseline."

Outside, Ben took a deep breath of the crisp autumn air and started toward the rear of the motel, stepping jauntily even as he realized that he'd never before applied the adverb "jauntily" to himself. If he started whistling a show tune, he'd really start to worry.

He had been skeptical, to say the least, about returning to Elderton to find the meaning and fame that had so easily and successfully eluded him all these years. Truth be told, even after he'd witnessed everything from a flickering superhero to a shambling dead girl, he still had no reason to believe that what he was searching for would turn up in his forgotten hometown.

Now things were different. Now life was shifting. Finally he'd taken the turn he needed to take. Finally he was driving down a road leading somewhere. Finally he was proving to himself that Ben Savitch was no longer the eternal left-blinker driver. He was hurtling toward shiny new destinations.

Stepping around the back corner of the motel, the circle of drinking newspeople came into view. He searched, but couldn't locate Max among the group and didn't recognize anyone else, so he thought he'd walk up and proudly introduce himself, let everyone know that they'd be witnessing the sight of their lives within mere hours, then let them toast him, one and all, raise a glass to the man who, having lifted an alien to the stars, had in the process lifted up all their lives.

Including his own, of course.

"Hey, buddy, you a newsman?"

It was an plump, unshaven guy who, for unknown reasons, wore a garish Hawaiian shirt, Bermuda shorts, and sandals while sitting outside drinking beer on a cool September afternoon.

The man pulled an icy beer from the cooler at his feet and thrust it into Ben's hand. "Join the party," he slurred, eyes affably unfocused. "Gonna be a good one."

Smiling, Ben popped open the beer and took several gulps. "I know it is. I'm—"

"You know," the man continued, "I have to hand it to good ol' Max Thomason. He gave us all the perfect excuse to have a great party away from the city, a little reunion of the regional affiliates. And it sure sounds like we'll get a fair sweeps story out of it, too. The way Max tells it, he's known this tabloid turdling for a long time—"

"But—"

"Wait, you gotta hear this." The man draped one ham-like arm over Ben's shoulder like they were Army buddies. "I watched Max filming his intro this morning. This Ben Savitch guy is a real lollapa-loser. He's spent his career chasing down dead-end stories and turning away from opportunities like they were rat poison. Well, this time he accidentally stumbled on the real thing and called Max, but told Max he thought it was a fake."

"But—"

"He has a genuine UFO, and a goddamned alien to boot! The alien communicates telepathically. Max heard it in his head! Tabloid boy didn't, at least the way Max tells it. I guess that the alien didn't think Savitch was an intelligent enough representative to beam thoughts to."

"But that's not tr—"

"Of course, Max will never admit to hearing alien voices on the air. Somehow he'll make Savitch the butt of the story, but why shouldn't he? To hear Max tell it, this guy wouldn't have even known the spacecraft was real if it hadn't been for him. Max was the one who realized what a find this was."

"But that's not tr—"

"Max said that Savitch just thought the thing was made of cardboard and tinsel, a certified fake, just like the way the rest of his cheesy stories have turned out. Shit, we're going to get footage of a real alien, a real UFO, and also a story about the blind idiocy of the tabloid press. If I wasn't a professional journalist, I'd almost feel sorry for this Savitch creep."

"But—"

"Max has promised us a liftoff at dusk. By this time tomorrow, all of us will be basking in the plums and kudos that were right under Savitch's nose all along, that only he could have been too retarded to see. What could be better? When we're done—zip!—we've got the first genuine UFO take-off footage filmed from multiple angles as well as a neat little story about tabloid papers and the nitwits who work for them. And all it cost us was two nights at a cheap motel. Hell, it only costs fifteen bucks to stay here, twelve-fifty if you make your own bed. Station management's gonna be mighty happy with all of us, getting a topnotch story on the cheap like this." The man stopped and took a swig of beer. "Life is good, ain't it, buddy?"

A hot lump smoldered halfway down Ben's throat. It wasn't moving.

"Say, buddy," the man said. "Who are you anyway?"

"I'm nobody," Ben said, turning away, tossing the beer can to the ground. "Don't you recognize me?"

Chapter Thirty-Eight

"Why did you come here?" Audrey asked.

Ben felt a gripping impulse to expound upon the virtues of the brand new Electrosux Vacuum Cleaner and its myriad flexible attachments.

She didn't want him in her home. Looking at her, it appeared that she might have been thinking that Ben would contaminate the premises with his toxic existence.

"I gave Chandler and Frank a ride home and noticed you had already gone, so I—"

"Almo woke up and asked us to leave. He wants to be alone, he said. I respected him enough to do that, which is more than I can say—"

"Audrey, please. I just came to tell you that if you want to come, the alien is taking off at sundown tonight, from behind the PrairieView."

Shaking her head, she said, "Why do you think I'd have the least bit of interest in that?"

Ben shrugged. "Because it's the only time in your life that you'll ever see a UFO take off, maybe?"

"I wanna go!" Jeffrey said, having overheard the conversation from the next room. He walked in smiling like there wasn't one thing wrong in the world. "I want to see how Mr. Quinn's repair worked. Perfect, I bet."

Nodding, Ben said, "I'm sure it'll be perfect. How did Chandler . . . I don't know . . . get healed like that? Who told him that the article about his death was a mistake?"

Jeffrey stood a little taller. "*I* wrote the correction. *I* saved him."

"How did you come up with that idea?"

Jeffrey shrugged, maintaining a cloak of mystery. "Just by thinking about things. My Mom always told me you could always do something at once, and that the best things you can do for people are the ones that you don't tell them you're doing for them. I did both of the things she always told me to do, and it worked."

"So you're keeping your healing powers secret?" Ben said, smiling, hoping that Audrey would take note of his warm attitude.

"You bet I am."

Frank Shepard, the fading Sky-Lord, ambled into the room. "Hello, Mr. Savitch."

It sounded like Frank was gargling through a throat tube. And now, when Ben looked closely, not only was Frank's image even more unstable, he was becoming translucent. Ben could see the wallpaper's flowered pattern through Frank's shifting image.

"What are you doing here?" Ben asked. "I just let you off at Chandler's house a few minutes ago."

"I thought I'd come over and visit with Jeffrey. I flew over here, without even crashing. I decided that maybe the only thing I'm going to contribute is some supportive fellowship to a youngster. I was always good with the children, as I remember."

Ben paused, then said, "What if I were to tell you that I have a better idea, that something occurred to me that might prove to be your ticket to the meaningful existence you've been aching for?"

Even though Frank's image was now violently fluttering and vacillating, Ben noticed the reanimated superhero's eyes widening, as well as his smile.

Audrey said, "Don't be making empty promises to Frank, Ben."

"I'm not. You'll just have to trust me on this."

"Right."

Ben gestured to Frank. "Come on with me, Frank. Let's take a walk. Audrey, Jeffrey, I'll be looking forward to seeing you tonight as the motel, okay?"

"Sure!" Jeffrey exclaimed.

Audrey said nothing, instead giving Ben a cursory nod, eyelids at half-mast.

Once outside, Frank said, "Where are we going?"

"We're going to take a little walk uptown. I do have to make one stop on the way, though."

"That's okay. It's a beautiful day." The excitement in Frank's sizzling voice was palpable. "Simply glorious," he wheezed.

They walked to the square, occasionally crossing paths with Eldertonians who nodded and smiled as if seeing an out-of-focus television star was nothing too unusual, not to mention encountering a man whose nosing around was destroying whatever fragile magic the town possessed.

As they neared the Rexall drug store, Ben pointed and said, "I need to stop in here a minute."

"No problem, Mr. Savitch. Whatever you say."

They entered. Ben spun the rack holding a colorful collection of comic books and—even though he noticed that their price had increased over a thousand percent since he'd last bought one—he politely purchased a recent release, rolled it up, and tucked it under his arm.

As they started to leave, the door almost slammed into Harold Brainard, who stood just outside.

Harold wasn't alone. Over his shoulder he carried a little girl. Although only her rear end and legs were visible, the gray-purple cast of her skin told Ben it was Vida Proust.

"Is she—?"

"She's asleep," Harold said. "I've been walking her around the square, telling her things."

"I see."

"I came here to touch the comic books. I think I'll be able to read one very soon."

"Oh, yeah? How's that?"

Harold leaned closer. Ben was surprised that his first inclination wasn't to pinch his nose closed and run for the hills. Harold seemed to have showered and brushed his paucity of teeth in the not-too-distant past.

"I know what happened," Harold said. "I know why I went blind."

Harold turned his head left to right as if to detect the approach of anyone he wouldn't want to hear what he was going to say. Then he continued, "I saw what happened to Almo and Chandler that night."

"The car wreck?"

"The car wreck. And you know what happened then?"

"What?"

"I ran out in the road. I saw the two of them lying on the ground, dead. I remember screaming, 'No! No! They're not dead! They're not dead!' and running back and forth between them. Then to myself I said, 'This isn't happening!' And then you know what happened?"

"You went blind," Ben said.

"Right! But not instantly. I can still remember that when my vision started to fade and even when the last images were melting away, the last thing I saw was Almo and Chandler starting to stir, starting to wake up, starting to live. When I found out that they'd been brought to life, I knew I couldn't let them know but I was always honest, have been all my life. So I did the next best thing."

"You forgot."

"Right. But that wasn't comforting, either. Not totally honest because I knew big chunks of my life were missing. So I kept looking for what I'd lost, what I'd forgotten. If I was searching, going somewhere, I was comforted, truthful. So I looked for people who could lead me, to help me find it all. People like you."

Nothing surprised Ben anymore in Elderton, certainly not this. "You had everything to do with Almo and Chandler living, didn't you? You had a lot to do with the magic in Elderton—"

"With them living, yeah. But not with the magic. That's been here all along. What I did was just . . . louder. I think it changed things."

"So if you remember everything now, why can't you see? I mean, what's the purpose of being blind anymore?"

Harold squinted, but his wandering, milky eyes were still visible. "You're right, I can see anytime I want to. I know that Chandler's recovered, but I don't think that even matters anymore. What matters is that I know what happened, know for sure. I think . . . hmm, I think I just need to wait for the right time. It's not like I'm in any hurry. You know, blindness has its virtues. I can tell you the name of a tree just by listening to the rustling of its leaves. I can tell you who's coming down the street just by breathing in their scent. I can tell you the mood of a bird by its song. I can tell you how long a fly has to live by the buzz of its wings. I can hear and smell a storm coming a day before anyone notices anything."

Ben was impressed. Besides gaining insight into what had happened to him, Harold also seemed to have gained about twenty I.Q. points in the process.

"You want to see something worth seeing, Harold?" Ben said. "How about coming to the motel tonight around dusk? I think you'll want to see what happens when the

UFO takes off. Once in a lifetime."

Harold shrugged. "Maybe. I'll see what I feel like."

Only in Elderton would someone think twice about witnessing the lift-off of an alien spacecraft.

"I also need to see what Vida needs, and if I can help her find it."

"What do you mean?"

"She needs light and warmth and faith and wonder."

"Yeah," Ben said. He reached out and touched the back of her leg. It felt like marble, hard and so cold. "I understand. Well, if you decide to come—both of you—I'll look forward to seeing you there."

Harold turned to enter the Rexall, apparently wanting to press his hands against the glossy covers of the comic books or to smell their pages.

Frank held open the door for them and, as Harold passed, Ben leaned down next to Vida's sleeping face and said, "I'm sorry."

Ben and Frank continued around the courtyard square, nodding to the passersby; even those in cars who waved as they watched Ben and Frank walking the crosswalk.

"Where are you taking me?" Frank finally asked. He'd been dying to ask, Ben knew, and had held himself in as long as he dared.

"Right this way, Frank," Ben said, opening the door to the public library.

Puzzled, Frank walked inside. "You want me to read something? A book?" he asked. "I don't think that's going to do anyth—"

"Not at all. There's someone here I want you to meet."

Ben took Frank by the arm—which now felt silky and insubstantial, like folds of a diaphanous robe—and escorted him to the front desk.

Ben breathed a sigh of relief when he saw the potential jungle temptress sitting at her desk, sewing. When she caught sight of Ben, she smiled her potential jungle temptress smile, a bit shyly, and stood up.

"Hello, again," she said with a wink, adjusting her cat-eye frames.

"Good afternoon, Mary Harmon," Ben said. Then he pulled Frank alongside him and said, "Mary, I'd like you to meet Frank Shepard, whom you may or may not know as Sky-Lord. Frank, this is the wonderful, gorgeous and gifted Mary Harmon. She's going to change your life . . . what there is of it."

Mary looked puzzled.

Ben smiled at her. This time, *he* winked.

Chapter Thirty-Nine

Max Thomason cleared his throat, then swept a hand over his gleaming head of wavy silver hair, smoothing it into a sculpted state of photogenic perfection.

The bright lights leapt to life.

Wally Fesler gave him the thumbs-up sign, then peered through the camera's viewfinder.

In a rich bass voice Max said, "Ready to go in five . . . four . . . three . . . two . . . one . . . Nestled in what Illinoisans have come to know as Forgottonia—West-Central Illinois—is the small community of Elderton. The town is known for nothing of significance: no local luminaries, past or present. No events of historical import. No major corporations or cultural centers. Elderton is what would politely be known as a sleepy little town. So why, you ask, is Max Thomason filing a report from this remote Midwestern hamlet? Simple. Tonight, in mere moments, a bona fide extraterrestrial spacecraft will be conveyed to this cornfield with its live alien occupant aboard, and will take off for the stars, the first such event ever to be filmed."

Max began walking slowly, dramatically—stiff, measured steps—as the camera followed him.

Eldertonians were arriving in droves: carloads of families, friends, neighbors, co-workers. No formal word had been circulated about tonight's event—no posters or newspaper items or radio announcements—but that didn't matter. Everyone knew what was going on in town, just as they always had and always would.

As the townspeople gathered, they politely remained behind Wally the cameraman as they watched Max's presentation. Most of them stood stoically: arms crossed, heads tipped to one side, neutral interest in the goings-on.

The other news crews were scrambling to and fro, making last-minute arrangements and adjustments, allowing Max the first go as they prepared themselves and their equipment for their own reports.

Waving his arm in a wide arc, Max announced, "We anxiously await the arrival of tabloid reporter Ben Savitch of *The Astonished Eye,* who originally stumbled upon the alien craft and its occupant, initially believing it to be an elaborate hoax, as all of the stories on which he's worked throughout his career have proven to be. Yes, it wasn't until much later—when your humble reporter arrived on the scene—that the importance and genuineness of his find became apparent."

Max stopped suddenly, flicked an index finger across his throat and said, "Cut! Okay, let's mark it here. If it turns out the thing is a hoax, we can burn the intro. If it's real, we keep it. Now when Savitch comes out and I interview him, I'm going into skeptic mode, Wally. That way, I'll cover us if it's a hoax. And if the craft turns out to be real, as I'm convinced it is, it'll be easy enough to edit out Savitch, leaving only *moi.* Got it, Wally?"

"Got it, Max."

Heads swept around. A few gasps were heard, but not many. Then a small smattering of applause commenced.

Max held one hand above his brow, dramatically peering through the increasing darkness. "I think he's coming, ladies and gentlemen."

Sure enough, around the far corner of the PrairieView motel walked Ben, with the teardrop-shaped UFO balanced on his back. The entity peered through the side portal of the craft, its face pressed flat against it.

The crowd opened to let Ben pass. Without saying a word, Ben walked through the bright lights, past Max and the camera, treading to the very edge of the cornfield and carefully setting down the craft.

Standing up, he brushed one hand against the other, turned toward the crowd, and smiled when he saw Audrey and Jeffrey standing there.

Audrey wore an expression of only mild interest on her face, although Jeffrey's eyes seemed as wide as the lemon moon that already had risen.

Jeffrey gave a little wave to Ben, who returned it.

The lights now trained on Ben, casting a long black shadow to the ground behind him.

The alien craft glimmered in the spotlights, throwing off an iridescent rainbow, muted hues changing with its every pulse.

Ben spied Harold in the crowd, standing alongside Vida Proust, holding her hand. Though she looked as rigid as lumber, she seemed mesmerized by the spacecraft. She let go of Harold's hand and took several spasming steps forward.

"Hi, Vida," Ben said. "I'm happy to see you here."

Motionless, her eyes remained glued to the UFO.

Ben returned to the side of the craft and patted its velvety hull.

Max walked up to Ben, either to share a thought or to make certain he was in camera range. "Are you ready, then?"

"Sure. Go ahead, Maxipad."

Whispering, holding his hand over the microphone, Max said, "Please, Ben, no nicknames while we're filming."

"Of course. You deserve the utmost respect. You're a professional, after all."

Pointing a microphone toward Ben's grim grin, Max

asked, "This, then, is the UFO, am I right?"

"That's right, Max."

"Where's it from?"

"I have no idea."

"Not even a guess? Care to speculate on what planet it represents? That's your job as a tabloid reporter, isn't it? Wild speculation?"

"No, I don't care to speculate. Thanks, anyway."

The craft was visibly pulsating, throbbing like a heart, its colors changing and whirling and shimmering with each beat.

"So when is it going to take off, Mr. Savitch? Do you have the flight schedule handy?"

"No, Max, I don't. Sorry. I think we've run into a problem."

"A problem? The pre-flight checklist revealed some engine problems? Perhaps they're related to that duct tape on the side of the spacecraft."

"No, it's not that. I had a conversation with the entity just moments ago—"

"You talk to the alien, too?"

"Well, kind of. It's telepathic communication."

"But of course." Max looked toward the camera and raised a perfectly groomed eyebrow.

"Anyway, the alien told me that it's not sure how to get to its home again. It's not sure which way to go when it takes off."

"So what are we waiting for? Contact with the control tower on Betelgeuse?"

"Nope. Here in Elderton, we have a better solution."

"What's that?"

Ben jerked his head skyward and pointed. "Sky-Lord! Master of the Elements!"

Above, appearing no larger than a jet at cruising altitude, a figure flitted across the darkening sky like a firefly, lit only by the moon's golden rays.

Max dropped the microphone to his side, craning his neck to get a better view.

After swooping through several aerial pirouettes and graceful barrel-rolls, the figure grew larger and larger as it approached.

"My God," Max said. "That *is* a person."

"Nope," said Ben, "not a person. Sky-Lord!"

When Frank Shepard—sans eyeglasses—was one hundred feet above the ground, the familiar costume came into view: the skin-tight body-suit of thunderhead gray, the chest emblem of a crescent moon in front of gathering clouds, the flowing magenta cape and matching boots.

Somewhere in the crowd, Ben knew, there was a deservedly proud potential jungle temptress librarian seamstress, her ample chest feeling full and warm as she witnessed the results of her rapid and picture-perfect needlework. Someday she would tell her lucky Tarzan about the day she'd sewn a Sky-Lord suit with only a comic book as her guide.

As Sky-Lord drifted slowly downward, to those present it became clear he was not alone. With his right arm he carried Chandler Quinn, whose face was beaming with pride at his reanimated Sky-Lord's realized potential. With his left arm Sky-Lord cradled Almo Parrish, who looked even smaller than he had the last time Ben saw him.

Sky-Lord's descent slowed, and he alighted gracefully on the ground next to Ben and Max.

Without pause, Chandler walked off to join Audrey and Jeffrey in the crowd.

Sky-Lord carried the dying Almo Parrish to a waiting

chaise lounge and laid him there so he could watch the activity in comfort, then returned to stand beside Ben.

Max's jaw had dropped open to a certifiably slack position. "Wha . . . that *is* Sky-Lord."

"Of course it is," Ben said. "He's the only one who can show the alien the way home. Isn't that right, Sky-Lord?"

Frank's exposed head and hands were rippling horribly now, almost transparent at times, so horribly Ben wondered if and how Sky-Lord would show up on videotape. Nevertheless, Sky-Lord smiled a wide, white, wavering grin, doubled his fists and jammed them against his hips, then crackled, "Mr. Savitch, that's what you led me to understand, that our friend from the stars is hopelessly lost. I'm more than happy to aid him in his quest to find his home. It's no trouble at all. That's why I'm here. That's what I do."

"Then I guess we're ready to go."

Ben noticed that cameraman Wally Fesler was trembling with either excitement or fear.

A voice boomed from the crowd. "Hold on a minute!"

An ashen-faced Max Thomason turned around yet again, shaking his head and gnarling his combed eyebrows as he watched the tall, lumbering figure of Harold Brainard approaching.

"I'm blind!" Harold exclaimed with a smile, turning toward the camera, leaning close to its lens and tugging his lower eyelids downward. "See my eyes? They aren't even pointing the same direction. You see?"

Leaning into Ben's shoulder, Max whispered, "What the hell is this?"

"Beats me, Max. Just another rube, I reckon."

Harold walked straight to Ben, then turned in Max's general direction. "You see my eyes, Mr. Newsman? Blind, aren't they?"

Max backed off a bit, sputtering. "Well, yes, yes they are."

Nodding, Harold said, "And I hear tell there's only one man in these parts who can help me to see again, and that man is Benjamin Savitch."

"What?" Ben said. This is the one thing he hadn't planned for tonight. He had no idea what to expect.

"Touch me, Mr. Savitch, lay your hands upon me. Please!" Harold postured like a hysterical Shakespearean actor.

Harold grabbed each of Ben's hands and pressed them to his sightless eyes.

Ben passively let it happen. *What the hell is this guy doing?* Moments of silence passed.

Harold let out a piercing cry, a howl, then fell writhing to the ground.

Ben and Max leaned down to see what was happening.

"Oh . . . my . . . God!" Harold shouted, casting his body left and right.

And then he rose to his feet, his gap-toothed smile as wide as the prairie, and screamed, "I can see, Mr. Savitch! I can see!"

Sure enough, Harold's eyes were not only focused straight ahead, directly at Ben, but they had lost their eerie milkiness. His eyes were a beautiful, shiny chocolate brown.

Harold fell to his knees, grabbing Ben's hands and kissing them.

The crowd applauded. Politely.

"How . . ." Max said, his face having lost the last vestige of professional indifference, "how in the hell did you do that?"

Ben shrugged, having no idea what had occurred. But he was an accomplished enough actor to play along. "Hey, what can I say? Maybe I have even more talents than you've given me credit for . . . Maxipad."

Helping Harold to his feet, Ben said, "Go on now, Harold, get out there with the crowd, see the people you haven't seen in years, and watch the magic."

"Yessir, Mr. Savitch, yessir, anything you say," Harold said, bowing and genuflecting as he walked backward. Before he'd completely lost himself in the crowd, he mouthed something to Ben. Luckily, Ben had gained some unwanted experience in deciphering Harold's speechless mouthings, and so understood: *I thought you needed that, maybe even deserved it. It's my gift to you. You're welcome.*

After acknowledging Harold with a smile and a nod, Ben said, "And now, Max, you'd better stand back. When Sky-Lord takes off, he's liable to stir up a little Midwestern soil."

"Uh, of course." Max was on automatic pilot now. He took a few shambling steps backward, resembling an extra in a zombie movie.

Ben walked to Sky-Lord and extended his hand. "I'm proud to have had the privilege to know you, Sky-Lord. Thank you for visiting us. If it weren't for you, this gentle creature from another world would be stranded on Earth forever. You're saving this little bundle of alien life, Sky-Lord, and in doing so, you're inspiring us all. I hope you're as proud of yourself as all of us are of you."

A tear slid from Sky-Lord's right eye, dangled from his blurring perfect jawline, then dropped glittering to the ground. "I'm proud to have known you, too. And Mr. Quinn and Mr. Parrish. I'm proud to have known Elderton. And I'm proud to help. That's what I'm here for. That's my job. That's what I do."

Ben touched an index finger to his forehead, like he'd

only now remembered something important. "Wait one minute, Sky-Lord. There's one more thing we have to do before you take off."

"Of course, Mr. Savitch."

Ben strode to Vida Proust and picked her up in his arms. Although she was stone-stiff, he tried to cradle her. Bending his head down, he whispered something into her ear, then turned his head to receive her labored reply.

He carried Vida to Phil and Elizabeth Proust—two loving parents whose bodies and souls had aged horribly with their daughter's lingering non-death—and spoke to them in hushed tones.

They stood there for several minutes, Phil and Elizabeth whispering to one another, hugging one another, then nodding.

"Are you sure, honey?" Elizabeth asked, stroking her daughter's hair.

"We love you more than all the stars in the sky, sweetheart," said Phil, kissing Vida's cold, small hand.

They each kissed Vida on the cheek, tidied up her muddy pink dress, and arranged her matted hair as best they could.

"With all she's been through," Elizabeth Proust said, "I think she deserves to do what she wants."

Nodding, Ben turned around and carried Vida to the spacecraft.

The entity had watched them approaching and a small hole appeared in the side of the craft, which then opened like a widening mouth in the gelatinous hull, until it was large enough to lay Vida inside, next to the lavender alien. The craft itself seemed to swell a bit to make room for the little dead girl.

The entity put its arm around her shoulders.

"If anyone knows where to find light and warmth and faith and wonder," Ben said, "I think it might be him . . . or her . . . or it. Travel safely, Vida, and dream well."

She tried to nod.

"Oh, and here's a gift for you, too, Mr. Alien." Ben explored his front pocket, then pulled out the photographs he had taken in the motel room. "Didn't you say that you wondered what you look like? Well, now you'll know. I won't be needing these."

The alien took the photos from Ben one by one, tipping its head left and right as it examined them.

Yes, it thought to Ben. *I recognize me.*

The hole closed like a rapidly healing wound, then sealed itself.

"Okay," Ben said, "we're ready."

He stood back.

Sky-Lord gazed heavenward, eyes searching the stars, scouring the sky for the perfect trajectory, crying eyes reflecting the light of the harvest moon.

He shouted in a strong, vibrant voice: "To the waiting stars!"

With that, Sky-Lord rose from the ground, slowly at first, slowly enough so the small spacecraft could arise and join him.

As the UFO ascended, the entity again pressed its face against the portal, its hand next to its head. Then Vida's head appeared next to the entity's. Although it was impossible to be certain, it looked like they were smiling.

Ben waved goodbye.

Max just stood there.

Sky-Lord's cries of joy and booming laughter echoed across the flat landscape as he rose impossibly fast into the night sky, followed closely by the teardrop-shaped spacecraft.

241

The crowd of Eldertonians, Ben, Max, and the cameras all trained their eyes on the ascending figures, watching as Sky-Lord led the UFO up through layers of wispy clouds.

"That's my boy!" Chandler yelled, slapping his thigh in glee. "Are you seeing this, Almo?"

From his place on the chaise lounge, Almo smiled weakly and slowly began to clap his hands. Soon the entire crowd joined him, the applause rising thunderously, filling the night.

And then, just as Sky-Lord had been reduced to a mere speck in the sky, he apparently lost his last hold on his fleeting existence. The wavering and flickering exacted their final toll on the reanimated Master of the Elements.

He exploded, but it wasn't an explosion in the destructive sense. Quite simply, he erupted in a luminous halo of light, an expanding blossom of brilliant colors whose individual petals trailed lazily downward toward the ground and the people of Elderton, illuminating the earth as the sparks drifted down and down and alighted on the soil and even the shoe-tops of those watching, before slowly dimming.

Everyone looked up again to see the entity's spacecraft wink out, embraced by the darkening sky.

Gone.

"Let me get this straight," Max said, eyes still pointed toward the heavens, "Sky-Lord led the alien craft to its homeward route . . . and then he exploded?"

"Gosh, I think you're right, Maxipad. Imagine that."

Without further ado, the citizens of Elderton began wandering away, the night having come to such gratifying closure.

"Wait!" Ben shouted. "Before you all go home, we need to acknowledge the presence of the man who made all this possible."

Max pointed to himself, questioning. Ben shook his head.

"Ladies and gentlemen," Ben continued, "for years the town of Elderton has enjoyed a simple, subtle magic that few walking this Earth have enjoyed. All of you know it so much better than I. For that, I envy you. But one person makes Elderton the most uncommon, loveliest place in the world. Not only has he made the coming of each autumn an unforgettable event, but he also has seen that no one who lived here ever forgets the rich legacy that is Elderton: its people. While he was repairing the spacecraft, Chandler Quinn told me about how this man—the last surviving Munchkin from *The Wizard of Oz*—developed the idea to create a special place that would house little pieces of Elderton's past so they could be experienced and enjoyed and revered by everyone, especially the children. You all know this place as the Presence Chamber.

"And now, as you all are aware, Almo is leaving us. He's reaching the period at the end of his sentence. He wants it that way. But even though he is not going to be predicting the first leaf to fall next autumn, he'll always be here with you. I think I'm telling you something you already know. But right here, right now, in front of these television cameras, I ask all of you to express your gratitude and your pride that you were permitted to walk the Earth when he did. Ladies and gentleman . . . Almo Parrish!"

Applause and cheers and two-fingered whistles. Even the news crews were clapping.

Before leaving, the Eldertonians walked to Almo, who lay barely conscious in the chaise lounge. One by one, they knelt next to him and laid their heads in his lap for a few seconds. He was weak, but he patted each one's head before they rose and departed.

It took a good thirty minutes for everyone to get his or her turn to honor Almo. Throughout that time, the cameramen kept filming, Max slouched with a vacant expression on his face, and Ben grinned. After everyone had paid respects, Chandler gently picked up his tiny friend and carried him away to take him home.

Approaching Ben, Audrey smiled that same smile that had captured his heart the first time he saw it. Jeffrey beamed ear to ear.

"You know something?" Audrey asked, reaching out and grabbing Ben's hands. "Tonight I think I saw a little bit of that wonderful first-grader."

"Thanks." He didn't know what else to say, so he left it at that.

"You did like my Mom always said to do, didn't you?" Jeffrey said. "You did Elderton a favor without letting anyone know about it. That's nice."

"Thanks, Jeffrey."

"Good night, Benny Savitch," Audrey said. She kissed him sweetly on the cheek, took Jeffrey's hand, and walked away.

Soon, the only humans remaining behind the PrairieView Motel were Ben and the newspeople.

Max scratched his head, dislodging a few lacquered silver hairs from their perfect resting places. "I don't think I even know what happened tonight."

"Gosh, that's a shame, Maximilian. Well, at least you've got it all on tape."

Wally Fesler whined, "This stuff is unusable! I mean, it was a nice show and everything, but we can't be broadcasting a piece in which a blind man is healed by a tabloid reporter, a dead girl takes a ride with an alien, and television's Sky-Lord flies into the sky and explodes. Who the hell would believe it? We'd all end up looking like idiots. Even—or *especially*—you, Max."

"He's right," Max said, shaking his head sadly. "I don't understand what happened here tonight, my friend, but the story is completely worthless."

Ben smiled. "Max, I can live with that."

Chapter Forty

"This is my last stop before leaving town," Ben said. "I've said goodbye to everyone else, paid my last respects to Almo."

"Is he still alive?" Audrey asked, stepping out her front door and standing on the stoop.

"Yes, but he's slipping away. He seems . . . well, he seems happier than *I've* ever been, to tell you the truth."

"How's Chandler holding up?"

"Pretty well, although his heart is breaking. But Chandler was still Chandler. In his case, of course, I couldn't just say goodbye; I had to bid him *adieu,* farewell, 'departing your comportment is such redolent anguish,' all of that."

"Are you sure you won't stay?" Jeffrey said, tugging at Ben's sleeve. "I think you'd be happy here."

"No, but thanks. I need to head back to Chicago, to see if I still have my job at the *Eye* when I show up without my big UFO story."

It was a cool day, but warm enough for shirtsleeves. The sun cast its gentle eye from a cloudless blue sky. Birds hymned, singing songs of lost summers and springs to come.

"It was wonderful what you did, Ben," Audrey said. "You surprised me in the best way."

"I think I surprised everyone. Including myself."

"It was very selfless of you."

Ben shrugged. "Maybe it was, by accident. But it was hearing what Max had planned for me, for himself, that sobered me up. So it was kind of selfish, too. I wanted a little poetic revenge. But I admit the whole thing felt pretty darned good, even the selfless stuff. Uniquely refreshing."

Audrey smiled. "It doesn't matter what route you took, Benny. What matters is that you ended up in the right place."

"I hope that happens someday, that I end up in the right place."

"Maybe Jeffrey had a point. What makes you think *this* isn't the right place?" Audrey asked. "You could always work for the *Elderton Pilot*, you know."

Ben laughed. "I don't think so. My specialty is obits and there doesn't seem to be much call for that particular skill around here."

Jeffrey said, "You could write one of those for Almo. He's dying . . . but he's happy, Ben. You don't need to worry about him."

"Thanks, Jeffrey. Maybe I will write something about Almo someday. If I do, I'll send you a copy."

Ben pulled Audrey close to him and gave her a long, gentle kiss on the cheek, then embraced her tightly while he said, "You know something? Meeting you has changed me so much. It helped me to remember what I want in a mate, more than anything."

Blushing, Audrey said, "What's that?"

"Someone who will hold my head in her lap or wipe my forehead with a cool washcloth when I'm dying. The rest is all just . . . decoration. You seem like that type of person, Audrey. I hope someday I'm worthy enough to spend my life with someone like you. I'm proud to know you. I'm proud you seem to like me a little bit."

"I do."

"And although I still don't feel I ever connected with

Elderton the way I expected, I hope I'm taking some of its magic home with me."

"Good."

"You know something else, Audrey? Just as you helped me remember something important, you helped me forget something, too, now that I think about it."

"What's that?"

"Darla."

"Who's Darla?"

"You don't want to know. Long story."

He bent down and gave Jeffrey a big hug and then, without another word, Ben Savitch got into his trusty rust-red Civic, waved goodbye, and drove away.

Of fortune he had little; of luck, he had more than he could have dreamed.

After waving good-bye to Ben, Audrey and Jeffrey sat on the front steps for a few moments, neither saying a word.

Jeffrey sighed.

"What wrong, Jeffrey? Something you need to say?"

"It's just that I thought he'd stay for sure," Jeffrey said. "I thought that was what he was meant for."

Drawing him close and patting his shoulder, Audrey said, "I guess we never know what people or things are meant for in this world, not for sure. That's what makes life interesting and exciting and fun. That's why it's so important to pay attention, so we can watch how things turn out."

"That's not what I'm talking about," Jeffrey said. He jammed his hand into his jeans pocket and pulled out a crumpled piece of newspaper. "When I was alone in the motel room, I looked through the stack of papers he'd brought from the library. I found this. I tore it out so he wouldn't see it."

Audrey took the ragged clipping from him, but she didn't need to read it. She knew, without looking, which article Jeffrey had found. It was a brief item, over thirty-five years old, about a six-year-old boy who, after a picnic with his first grade classmates, had fallen into a rock quarry and drowned.

"You knew?" Jeffrey asked.

Audrey nodded. "I was there. With Miss Harnaker and a couple of the other children, I helped pull him out of the water."

"He died right then?"

"No, but soon. But not for very long." She sighed, furtively wiping a tear from her eye. "He had his head in my lap when he died . . . *and* when he woke up. I stroked his hair."

"Gosh, and he didn't remember any of it. I bet you were surprised when he showed up in town."

Audrey nodded. "People in town warned his family not to leave. That had never happened before as far as I know, someone being hoped to life and then moving out of town. I'd always assumed he hadn't lived long."

Jeffrey fell silent for a moment, then said, "Do you think he'll come back?"

"I don't know."

"Well, we can hope."

"That's right, Jeffrey. That's our secret. That's our magic. We can hope."

Chapter Forty-One

Ben decided to take one last leisurely drive around the courthouse square before leaving town. He didn't know if, while he walked the planet, another opportunity would ever come for him to see a place so ordered and gorgeous and peaceful, and he wanted to soak it all in, to store every last detail as deeply as possible in his mind. If nothing else, perhaps in the future his memories of Elderton would help him fall to sleep at night.

He had just pulled onto the square when a lone golden leaf landed on his windshield, directly in front of his eyes, and lay there trembling.

He pulled into a parking space and turned off the engine. Smiling to himself, Ben opened his window and reached around to grab hold of its stem, then brought it inside and gazed at it. The perfect memento of his days in Elderton.

Lying in his hands, the leaf embodied all the beauty and sadness in the world, with its flaxen heart and its ridge of deepening scarlet.

He looked up again, surprised to find his vision wavering as tears pooled in his eyes. That instant, Ben Savitch witnessed something as strange and magical as everything else he had seen in his forgotten hometown.

The leaves began falling from all the trees in the square— the towering oaks, the majestic maples, the glorious elms— and not just falling one by one.

They fell at once, together.

Disbelieving at first, he opened his car door and stepped out into the sunshine. He looked around. The few people walking the square had stopped, each eyeing the wondrous display, each smiling.

Within seconds the sky was entirely filled with burnished leaves of red and gold and orange, each one spinning contentedly in its own dance to the waiting Earth.

Ben stepped onto the curb and into the courtyard. Leaves gathered around his feet.

"Almo," he whispered.

Although he did not possess the powers that many in Elderton did, Ben did not have to wonder long to conclude what had happened.

Thousands of leaves falling as one, drifting toward the ground, thicker than a blizzard.

Almo Parrish—the last Munchkin—had died.

Ben listened to the gentle whispers of the falling leaves as they grazed one another, buffeted about by the warm breeze. For a fleeting moment, he held the thought that he could be blamed for Almo's death. But then, reviewing his brief time in Elderton, he was confident that wouldn't happen. No.

The sky remained awash with pirouetting leaves now blocking out the sky, the sun, the clouds, the people standing on the sidewalks, the mother trees themselves.

He didn't know whether to feel relief or guilt or sadness or joy, so he felt them all.

The air before him was a brilliant, fluttering fog of blazing color, impossible for vision to penetrate.

He smiled as he stepped back to his car and opened the door, eyes lingering on the courtyard—now completely blanketed with radiating color—and the continuing earthward dance of the leaves that descended *en masse* to pay silent, vivid tribute to the tiny Munchkin who had honored them for so many years.

Taking a deep breath, Ben got into the car and reached toward the glove compartment so he could find his road map and trace a route back to the city while he was waiting for the last leaf to fall. If nothing else, perhaps studying the map would anchor him to reality again, would help him adjust to the fact that he would soon be leaving so much behind, most of which he decided he would not be able to understand, or even name, for many years to come.

A small corner of fabric dangled from the corner of the glove compartment's door.

Feeling furrows of puzzlement wrinkling his forehead, he opened the glove compartment. Inside was a bundle of cotton fabric, cheery Play-Doh green. He lifted it out. Something was wrapped inside it.

Carefully, Ben unfolded the green cloth. Out dropped an object about the size and shape of a paperback book.

He held it in his hand, turned it over. The substance shimmered and pulsed and glowed with glistening, iridescent colors.

"I'll be damned," he said aloud. "A piece of the spacecraft."

Someone had gifted him with the one thing he needed to make his story a reality: irrefutable physical evidence of a crashed UFO.

He spied a small note lying on his passenger seat. On it was written, in grand bold letters:

I envisaged you enjoying
the possession of this precious and peerless artifact.
Do with it what you will.
Live well, my existential compadre.
Best wishes, Chandler

He let his thumb play over the silky texture of the fragment, allowing the feel of the impossibly light, velvety substance to register. He wanted to remember this, too.

Then Ben rolled down the passenger window and let the fragment fly, hurling it with a sharp flick of the wrist so that it sailed a great distance through the air, finally landing among the gathering leaves in the center of the courtyard.

Soon a child would discover the fragment, perhaps, and feel like he or she had stumbled upon the greatest treasure ever. Or an old man might come across it, taking it to Duane and Joyce's Coffee Shop so the patrons could talk and laugh about it all morning. Or perhaps a happy dog would find and bury it, keeping it safe and forgotten in the Earth.

Ben felt very good.

He started to wad up the green cloth when he noticed something else.

A tiny paper note was safety-pinned to it.

He looked closer.

The tag read, in faded ballpoint: "Benjamin Avery Savitch. September 16, 1958. Age 4."

He began crying even before he leaned his head back against the headrest and pressed the tiny swath of the little boy's muscle shirt to his face, breathing in the aromas of chalkboard dust and Mom's perfume and a newly oiled baseball glove, of mimeograph ink and puppy breath and Vicks Vapo-Rub and sunshine-warmed sidewalks, of burning leaves and new school clothes and sports card bubblegum and hot chocolate chip cookies and Dad's Vitalis.

He stepped out of the car and walked onto the courtyard, then lay down upon the thick cushion of autumn leaves, feeling the breeze playing over his body, seeing the warm sky opening above him.

He held the cloth tightly to his face and inhaled as deeply as he could.

It was there:

The fragrance of summers and play . . . and innocence and wonder.

And life.

Most of all, life.

> "an intuition remains,
> of surrenders to be made,
> and of places made different
> by the emptiness embraced."
> —Author unknown

About the Author

Tracy Knight's short fiction has appeared in numerous anthologies in a variety of genres, including suspense, mystery, science fiction and horror. He is also the author of a western novel, *Beneath a Whiskey Sky*. His nonfiction, primarily focusing on psychological topics, has included a chapter in the Writer's Digest book *Writing Horror* and a column for *Mystery Scene Magazine*.

Tracy, his wife Sharon, and three feline life forms live in rural west-central Illinois, where he works as a clinical psychologist and university professor.